I just want to hold him," Aidan said. My little brother leaned around me and reached for the dog again.

Suddenly the dachshund went "RARF! RARF!" very loudly right in Aidan's face.

Startled, Aidan jumped back and fell over on his butt. The dog wriggled around in my arms, licked my neck, and looked back at Aidan like, *Yeah, and stay out!*

I felt a little bad about the bewildered look on Aidan's face, but I also felt a terrific explosion of happiness inside me. The dog had chosen *me* over sweet, adorable Aidan. That *never* happened.

"Everything OK here?" Mom asked, coming back over to us.

"Yup," I said, rubbing the dog's head. "Everything's perfect."

I had no idea how wrong I was.

Get into some

Pet Trouble

Runaway Retriever

Loudest Beagle on the Block

Mud-Puddle Poodle

Bulldog Won't Budge

Oh No, Newf!

Smarty-Pants Sheltie

Bad to the Bone Boxer

Dachshund Disaster

Pet Trouble

Dachshund Disaster

by T. T. SUTHERLAND

SCHOLASTIC INC.

New York   Toronto   London   Auckland

Sydney   Mexico City   New Delhi   Hong Kong

No part of this publication may be reproduced, stored in a retrieval system, or transmitted in any form or by any means, electronic, mechanical, photocopying, recording, or otherwise, without written permission of the publisher. For information regarding permission, write to Scholastic Inc., Attention: Permissions Department, 557 Broadway, New York, NY 10012.

ISBN 978-0-545-20272-5

12 11 10 9 8 7 6 5 4 3 2 1   10 11 12 13 14 15/0

Printed in the U.S.A.   40
First printing, April 2010

For Charlie and Sam ☺

CHAPTER 1

Nobody likes my older brother except his dog.

I mean, my mom will tell you she likes him, and if you get my little brother, Aidan, to look up from his dinosaurs for a minute, he'll say David is OK by him, but I don't really believe them.

David is just like his dog, Bowser. They both have short black hair. They both growl at anyone who comes near them. They both like to shut the door and stay up in David's room all the time. They're both kind of pudgy around the middle because they would rather lie around and watch TV than do anything else. They even both have freckles, although David's are the normal kind, while Bowser's are just spots of brown fur on his long black face.

It makes sense that they like each other so much. They sure don't like anyone else! David picks on me and Aidan all the time, and he fights with Mom over just about everything. He won't let us in his room, he won't let us talk to his friends, and he won't let us even try to play with his dog. Not that we would want to — stupid Bowser would probably bark us out of the room if we went anywhere near him.

Bowser is a big, grumpy mutt with droopy black ears and a tan underbelly. He was a lot cuter when he was a puppy. I don't really remember, because I was only four, but I've seen the photos of the Christmas when Dad gave Bowser to David. David was seven. (He was a lot cuter then, too.)

That was the last Christmas before Dad died. He knew he was sick, and so did Mom, but they didn't tell us until he had to go into the hospital a couple months later. I guess it was something he had for a long time and they didn't know exactly how long he would be around for, so they didn't want us to worry about it. But we all got to say good-bye — there are photos of that, too, of each of us sitting on the hospital bed with Dad and him smiling like he loves each of us the best.

I wish I remembered him better. I remember scratchy cheeks when he hadn't shaved and a big deep laugh and his voice reading *Where the Wild Things Are* to me over and over again because I loved it so much.

Other than that, all I know is that he liked dogs, because he looks like he's laughing a lot in the photos with Bowser and David. I would ask Mom to tell me more about him, but that always makes her look really sad. My friend Midori asked me once if Mom ever goes out on dates, but she doesn't — she's too busy with work and us, and I think she still misses Dad. Maybe I could ask David what he remembers, if he weren't so grumpy all the time.

I know Aidan wouldn't be any help, because he remembers even less than I do. The Christmas when we got Bowser was also Aidan's first Christmas with us. He's beaming in all the photos — Aidan's first stocking, Aidan's first snowman, Aidan's first candy cane. He looks like everything in the world makes him happy. You can see why Mom and Dad adopted him. When they went to Cambodia, they were actually planning to get a little girl, but once they saw Aidan, they couldn't resist him. He just has one of those faces.

He's still like that now, six years later. He's pretty much the opposite of David — all smiles and hugs and giggles. When Mom got us a Maine coon kitten two years ago, it was supposed to be for the whole family, but the cat fell for Aidan just like everybody else does, so it's pretty much his now. He even got to pick the name, which if you ask me wasn't such a great idea, because now we've got Bowser the mutt and . . . Meowser the cat. I know, my friends all think that's pretty hilarious. Because Aidan is just *so* cute.

And then there's me. I'm the one in the middle. I'm not mean and smart like David, or cuddly and cute like Aidan. I'm just Charlie.

When we walk in the door after school, this is what happens: Bowser runs over and jumps up on David, wagging his tail frantically as if he thought David would never come home. Meowser slinks over more slowly and curls around Aidan's legs, purring loud enough for the whole neighborhood to hear.

Nobody says hi to me at all.

That's why this year I told my mom that instead of a party, I wanted a dog of my own for my tenth birthday. I wanted a dog that would be all mine — one I could keep away from David the way he keeps Bowser away from us. I wanted a dog who would like me as much as Meowser likes Aidan. I wanted a dog who'd be mine and nobody else's.

You know what they say: Be careful what you wish for. . . .

CHAPTER 2

My birthday didn't start off well. Maybe that should have been a warning sign.

First I was woken up by my bedroom door banging open.

"Hey brat," David said from the doorway. "Mom says to get up or you'll miss your birthday breakfast."

"Rrrrruff," Bowser agreed, sticking his nose around the corner to glare at me.

"Not that I care," David said. "More for me, ha-ha. So stay in bed if you want to. Whatever." He turned around and stomped back down the stairs with Bowser trotting at his heels.

I sat up, rubbing my eyes, and looked over at Aidan's side of the room. Of course he was already awake and gone. He gets up at the crack of dawn and sits outside Mom's room, reading one of his dinosaur books, until she wakes up. She thinks this is because he likes to give her a hug first thing in the morning. I think it's because he wants to make sure she doesn't spend one moment of time away from him.

It was only nine a.m., which made it kind of weird that David was awake, too. Normally on the weekends he sleeps as late as he can — or at least, he stays in his room most of the morning and only comes down for lunch. I guess the smell of something more than cereal for breakfast lured him out this once, like a mean old bear coming out of his cave all hungry and grumpy.

I hunted around the room for my favorite shirt, but I couldn't find it. I was sure I'd put it on the chair the night before so I could wear it for my birthday. But it was nowhere to be found. Finally I put on jeans and a long-sleeved orange-and-white shirt, combed my reddish-brown hair until the waves went in the right direction, and went downstairs.

Aidan was setting the table in the kitchen while Mom was busy at the stove. He looked up and gave me one of his angelic smiles as I came in.

"Happy birthday, Charlie!" he cried.

My mouth fell open. "Aidan!" I said. "That's *my* shirt you're wearing!"

He looked down at himself with a puzzled

expression. Except he couldn't have been all that puzzled, because not only was it too big for him, the shirt actually said CHARLIE across the front in big green letters. I mean, come on!

"Oh," he said. "Oops! That's so funny!" He started cracking up.

"I want it back!" I said. "I was going to wear that today!"

"Well, good morning to you, too, Prince Charming," Mom said, coming over and kissing me on the head.

"Tell Aidan to give back my shirt," I said.

"Can't I wear it just for today?" Aidan asked. "Please? In honor of your birthday?"

I gave Mom a look and she sighed. "He did say 'please,'" she pointed out. "Could we start off the day without fighting?"

"Oh, fine," I said, although it wasn't really fine because I'd been waiting all week to wear that shirt on my birthday, and now it would have to go in the laundry and I wouldn't get to wear it again until whenever the laundry was done. Aidan ran over and hugged me, which made Mom smile.

"What a good brother you are," she said to me. "I can't believe you're already ten. When did that happen?" She went back to the stove, retying her sunshine-yellow apron.

"I'll be eight soon!" Aidan announced. "Two more weeks!"

"That's true!" Mom said with another smile. "I hope you've started thinking about what you want for your birthday."

"Whatever you want to give me," Aidan said sweetly. "And some more dinosaur books," he added quickly. Aidan has already decided he's going to be a paleontologist when he grows up. He says he's going to discover a new species of dinosaur and name it after whichever of us he loves most that day, or maybe all of us . . . *Momocharliesaur davidrex.*

I think being a paleontologist sounds kind of boring. I imagine it involves a lot of digging in the dirt and cleaning old bits of rock all day to see if they're bones. Dinosaurs are cool enough, but paleontology? Yawn.

I'm going to be an astronaut. Doesn't that sound much cooler? I'm going to ride rocket ships into space and see the Earth from far away and be the first person on Mars. That's my plan, anyhow. Mom thinks it's a great idea. She says I should work hard at science and math to make sure I can get into astronaut school one day. She even said she might let me go to space camp one summer if I keep my grades up.

Since I can't actually start training to be an astronaut yet, mostly what I do now is draw pictures of spaceships and rockets and planets and stuff. We covered my school books in brown paper this year so I could draw on them as much as I want, and they're all full of rockets already. There are little astronauts and moons in all the corners of my notebooks, too.

My art teacher, Mrs. Bly, has tried to get me to draw other things besides spaceships and aliens, but I'm like, why would anyone want to draw a bowl of fruit when they could draw a *rocket* instead? Right?

My sketch pad was lying open on the table, which meant Aidan had probably been looking at it. He's still too young for the after-school art class I'm taking, but I know he'll want to be in it next year, so that's when I'll stop taking it. I see him enough at home; the last thing I need is *more* time with my little brother.

I closed the sketch pad and put it in my backpack by the door, which I'm pretty sure is where it was originally. Aidan, in case you can't tell, has a really wobbly idea of what "privacy" means. He goes into my stuff all the time, and what am I supposed to do about it? We share a room, so it's kind of impossible to stop him.

David stomped into the kitchen and threw himself into a chair at the table. He was wearing a black T-shirt and faded dark blue jeans, like he always does. "Let's get this over with," he grumbled. I guess he had some really important video games waiting for him back in his room or something. Bowser crawled under his chair and flopped down with a noisy sigh.

"Here, put these on the table," Mom said, handing a plate to Aidan. It was stacked high with French toast.

"French toast?" I said. "What happened to pancakes?"

Mom looked flustered. "I thought you wanted French toast," she said.

"I like pancakes better," I said. "I've *always* liked pancakes better. That's why we *always* have pancakes on my birthday and French toast on *Aidan's* birthday."

"Everybody knows *that*," David said, but in this mean, sarcastic way where he was actually picking a fight with Mom and making fun of me at the same time.

Mom wiped one hand across her forehead. "I'm sorry, Charlie, I forgot," she said.

Aidan looked innocent, but I could guess what really had happened. Mom probably asked him what she should make for breakfast, and he voted for French toast, like he always does. She didn't even think about what *I* would want.

Giovanni never makes these mistakes. He's kind of our nanny, although we don't call him that because we're too old to need a nanny anymore. He picks us up after school every day and drives us to activities and does all the housework and takes care of the pets during the day and hangs out with us whenever Mom's at work. Mom loves it because she can focus on her work, and she says she likes that we have a "good male role model" around, whatever that means. Giovanni would have remembered that I like pancakes best, but of course it was Sunday, so he was at his own house, probably studying for one of his online college courses.

"Well, you're ten now," Mom said, "so I'm sure you're old enough to handle a different kind of exciting birthday breakfast, right?"

David rolled his eyes and pulled out his cell phone. He started pressing buttons in that way that means he's texting his friends. I think it's mysterious that anyone would be friends with David, but I guess there's someone who doesn't mind texting with him, anyway.

"Charlie?" Mom said hopefully.

"All right," I said. "It's fine." It wasn't fine. French toast is too eggy for me, and I don't like eggs. But if I took the pieces with the least egg and covered them in maple syrup, I could sort of pretend they were pancakes.

"Can I get you something to drink?" Aidan offered. "Milk? Orange juice? Hot chocolate?"

"That's very sweet of you, Aidan," Mom said, patting his head.

"Mrrrrrroww," Meowser agreed from the top of the refrigerator.

"It's OK, I'll get it," I said.

"Orange juice," David said without looking up from his phone, even though Aidan totally hadn't been talking to him.

Aidan accidentally got in my way while I was trying to get the milk out and I nearly poured it all over him. Maybe Meowser could tell I was a little mad at Aidan, because she hissed at me and lashed her tail, which made Bowser lift his head up and growl.

I had that feeling I always get: that no one in the

room really likes me, except maybe Aidan, but he's nice to everybody so it hardly counts.

"So!" Mom said, trying to sound cheerful as we all sat down at the table. She'd put a vase of fire-colored chrysanthemums, dark red and gold, in the middle of the pale orange tablecloth. Her flowers in the garden are basically her favorite thing in the world; she spends half of every weekend out there taking care of them.

She spread her napkin on her lap. "Who wants to come meet this dog with me and Charlie?"

That cheered me up right away. In all the stupidness about my shirt and the French toast, I'd nearly forgotten we were going to get me a dog today.

"I do!" Aidan shouted, waving one hand in the air.

David rolled his eyes again. "Not if you paid me," he muttered.

"David, no texting at the table," Mom said for maybe the five hundredth time. They have this fight constantly, but I kind of think it's her own fault for getting him a phone, especially one with unlimited texting. He gave her a stony look, then turned off the phone and shoved it in his pocket.

"Where's the dog?" Aidan asked through a mouthful of French toast. "What kind of dog is it? What's its name? How did you find it?"

"We found it on a website called Petfinder," Mom said. "It's at a foster home not far away. And it's a dachshund, just like Charlie wanted."

"One of those stupid sausage dogs?" David snorted. "Figures."

"He's really cute," I said to Aidan, ignoring David. "He's only a year old, and he was abandoned with his brothers and sisters. He's the last one left without a home. And they said I could name him whatever I want."

"Let's call him Yowser!" Aidan shouted. "So he'll match Bowser and Meowser!"

"No!" I said. "No way!"

Aidan gave me a wounded expression. "Why not?" he said. "It'd be cute."

"Barf," David said without looking up from the food he was shoveling into his mouth. "Lamest idea ever." Which is maybe the only time I've ever agreed with him about anything.

"I think it'd be cute, too," Mom said, jumping in before Aidan could start crying. "But Aidan, this is Charlie's dog, so he gets to pick the name, all right?"

"OK," Aidan said, pushing his fork around the plate. "I still think Yowser would be cute, though," he muttered.

"He better not eat Bowser's food," David said. "Bowser won't like that. He better stay out of Bowser's way."

"That's the plan," I said. I wanted my dog to stay far away from Bowser and David. David is the kind of person who would kick a small dog if he got the chance, and Bowser only pays attention to other dogs long enough to growl at them until they run away.

"Maybe he can be friends with Meowser instead," Aidan offered.

I didn't want that to happen, either. I definitely didn't want my dog to get along with Aidan and Meowser better than with me. It worried me that Aidan was even coming with us to meet him.

"Mom, I'm done," I said, pushing away my plate. I was still hungry, but I didn't want any more egg-tasting French toast.

"All right," Mom said, putting down her napkin and beaming at me. "Let's go meet this dog!"

CHAPTER 3

I was nervous as we rang the doorbell at the dog's foster house. The dachshund was really cute in the photo online, but what if he was weird in real life? What if he was hyper or boring or crazy? Or worse, what if he didn't like me at all?

Immediately there was a volley of loud, high-pitched barking from inside. It sounded like more than one dog. Mom rubbed her purse strap anxiously. "I hope that's not *our* new dog making all that noise," she joked.

We're not used to noisy dogs in our house. Bowser never barks at the doorbell or the mailman or people coming in. At most he'll stand at the top of the stairs and growl. He only barks sometimes at other dogs, like if he sees them across the street from our yard.

An old man in a pink plaid sweater vest opened the door and smiled at us. "You must be the Graysons," he said. "I'm Milton Schwartz — come in, come in."

"My name is Aidan," Aidan announced with a big smile as he stepped inside. "Nice to meet you, sir." He held out his hand for Milton to shake, so then of course I had to do that, too. Aidan can be a little weird and old-fashioned like that with grown-ups, but Milton seemed to like it.

"Ruthie, they're here!" he called. We could still hear barking from the back rooms.

"Uh — how many dogs do you have?" Mom asked.

"Seven at the moment," Milton said. "Three of our own and four that we're fostering until they find good homes. We just can't resist their little faces, and since our kids moved out, it sure keeps us busy." He grinned as his wife came into the room. She had silver hair pinned into a loose bun and a pink tracksuit that matched his sweater vest.

She was carrying the most handsome dog I'd ever seen.

"Oh!" Aidan cried, pressing his hands to his chest dramatically.

The dachshund had floppy brown ears and a long brown body with short fur and little stubby legs. His black eyes were shining and alert, darting from my mom to me to Aidan and back again.

"We've been calling him Chutzpah," Milton said. The way he said it sounded like "Hoots-pah." "Ruthie says it's very appropriate for such a bold, nosy little dog!"

I looked at Mom and she laughed politely, although I don't think she completely understood the joke either. It didn't matter, though; I would definitely be changing his name — just as soon as I thought of one that was perfect for him.

"Which of you is Charlie?" Ruth asked, smiling at us.

I waved, and she beckoned me over. We both knelt on the floor and she set the dog down between us. I held out my hand and he sniffed it really thoroughly with his long nose, starting at my fingertips and going down to my wrist and then back up my thumb.

"Here," Ruth whispered, passing me a dog treat. "These are his favorites."

I held out the treat and his tail swooshed up and started wagging. He looked up into my face and opened his mouth a bit like he was smiling.

"Sit," I said. I'd been watching *The Dog Whisperer* and *It's Me or the Dog* nonstop for a week, so I knew you were supposed to make the dog do something to earn its treat each time.

But the dog just kept looking at me, and Ruth and Milton both laughed. "Good luck with that!" Milton said. "We've been trying for a month and it's pretty much impossible to teach him anything."

"Impossible?" Mom said in a worried voice.

"Oh, but he's house-trained!" Ruth reassured her. "We figured that was the most important thing."

"Sure," Mom said. "Yes. True." She tucked a strand of red hair behind her ear and studied the dog.

The dachshund's tail was still wagging. His sharp black eyes were fixed on the treat now. I didn't know what else to do, so I just gave him the treat. His ears flapped as he chomped it down and then licked my fingers.

"Dachshunds are like that," Milton added. "Stubborn, but very cute."

"And very loyal," Ruth said. I liked the sound of that. I wanted my dog to be loyal to me more than anything.

The dachshund suddenly took a step forward and planted his front paws on my knees. He leaned up toward my face with his tail wagging.

"Wow," Milton said. "He likes you!"

"He's usually much more nervous around strangers," Ruth said admiringly.

I grinned at the dog. Slowly, so I wouldn't startle him, I reached out and stroked his smooth head and back. His tail wagged even harder. His fur was short and a little oily under my fingers. I felt like I could sit there and pet him forever.

"This looks like a match to me!" Ruth proclaimed.

Milton started talking to my mom about the paperwork while Ruthie went to get a bag of things for the dog. I scratched behind the dachshund's long, shiny ears. He pulled himself all the way into my lap and sat down.

"Can I say hi?" Aidan asked suddenly from behind me, and the dog and I both jumped. Without waiting for an answer, Aidan was already reaching for the dog's face. "Hi dog! Can I hug him, please, can I?"

"I don't think he'd like that," I said, trying to shift away from Aidan's grasping hands.

"I just want to hold him," Aidan said. He leaned around me and reached for the dog again.

Suddenly the dachshund went "RARF! RARF!" very loudly right in Aidan's face.

Startled, Aidan jumped back and fell over on his butt. The dog wriggled around in my arms, licked my neck, and looked back at Aidan like, *Yeah, and stay out!*

I was afraid Aidan would start crying, but I guess he was too surprised to cry. I mean, pretty much no one ever yells at him, and usually animals love him. I felt a little bad about the bewildered look on Aidan's face, but I also felt a terrific explosion of happiness inside me. The dog had chosen *me* over sweet, adorable Aidan. That *never* happened.

"Everything OK here?" Mom asked, coming back over to us.

"Yup," I said, rubbing the dog's head. "Everything's perfect."

I had no idea how wrong I was.

CHAPTER 4

There were a couple of warning signs. As we left the house with me holding the dog on a short red leash, Ruth said, "Oh, I forgot to ask. You don't have any other pets, do you?"

Mom hesitated, like she was afraid they'd take the dog back if she told the truth, but of course she's Mom, so she did anyway. "We do, actually," she said. "A dog and a cat."

"Oh," Ruth said, chewing on her bottom lip. "Well, you might want to keep them apart as much as possible. We've been keeping Chutzpah in my sewing room by himself most of the time. He's . . . not particularly fond of other animals. But I'm sure he'll warm up to yours eventually!"

"Call us if you have any problems," Milton said. "If anything goes wrong, we'd rather take him back than have you give him to a shelter."

"Nothing will go wrong," I said. The dog had buried his nose in a clump of purple flowers by the door and was pawing at the dirt curiously.

"Thanks very much," Mom said. "We'll keep you posted." Milton and Ruth waved as we walked back to the car.

Aidan had been really quiet since the dog barked at him. He didn't even ask if he could sit in the front seat on the way home. The dog stood on my lap with his front paws up on the door and peered out the window for the whole drive. I rubbed his back and sometimes he'd turn and look at me like he was checking that it was still me patting him.

We could hear loud music thumping from David's room when we opened the front door to our house. The dachshund twitched his ears and looked around in this cute, confused way.

"David!" my mom shouted up the stairs, but of course he couldn't hear her. "Aidan, go get your brother while I make lunch," she said.

Aidan bounded up the stairs and I followed Mom through the living room to the kitchen. The dachshund trotted at my heels, his ears flapping as he whipped his head in every direction, trying to sniff everything at once.

"What would you like for lunch?" Mom asked. I knew that was her way of saying she still felt bad about making the wrong thing for breakfast.

"Grilled ham and cheese?" I suggested.

"Excellent choice," she said with a smile. She got out the bread and started slicing cheese while I put down food and water for the dog on the far side of the refrigerator. I was pretty proud of the new dog dishes we'd bought for him: red, with little white dog bones on them. They looked very cool next to his shiny brown coat and red collar.

But the dog couldn't have been less interested in them. The dachshund sniffed his food, gave me a dubious look, and then trotted across the kitchen to the mat where Bowser's empty metal food dish sat next to his water bowl. I'd given him the same food Bowser gets, but he spent ten minutes sniffing Bowser's dish anyway, as if he suspected there was something better hidden in there somewhere.

Finally he licked it clean, then lifted his head, sniffed, and followed his nose around the kitchen table to the corner where Meowser's food and water were set out in these little matching fish-shaped ceramic containers.

There was still food left in Meowser's dish — she's kind of a fussy eater. So I hurried over and picked it up before the dog could eat any of it.

"Uh-uh, no," I said. "No cat food for you. Gross. Yuck. No."

The dog gave me a look like, *You dare deny ME something I want?* If he'd had eyebrows, one of them would have been raised skeptically. But when I wouldn't put the dish back down, he turned and strolled back to his own food again. I loved the way he held up his head proudly, as if he was surveying his kingdom while he walked.

"What are you going to name him?" Mom asked.

"Something noble," I said. "Like Sheriff or Duke or Prince or Rajah."

Unfortunately, David came into the kitchen just in time to hear me say that. He laughed in his smirky, unfriendly way. "Rajah?" he echoed. "Sheriff! Those are the dumbest —"

"Rarf! Rarf! Rarf!" the dachshund suddenly yapped, noticing David for the first time. "RARF!" His bark was a lot louder and deeper than I would have expected from such a little guy. He looked at me as if making sure he had backup, then whipped his head back around to David. *"RARF! RARF!"*

"Uh, someone is loud," David observed snidely, crossing his arms.

I heard nails skidding on the living room floor and realized that Bowser was running after David to find out what all the barking was about. I tried to grab the dachshund, but he bounced out of my reach just as Bowser burst into the kitchen.

"RARF RARF RARF RARF RARF!" the dachshund hollered angrily. He wasn't at all afraid to get in Bowser's face, although Bowser was at least four times his size.

Bowser growled, showing his teeth. His paws were planted squarely on the kitchen tile, and his small eyes shifted from the dachshund to me to his food dish. He stepped forward menacingly, placing himself between my dog and David.

The minute he moved, the dachshund went berserk. *"RARF RARF RARF RARF RARF RARF RARF RARF RARF!"* he yelled, running at Bowser and then darting back at the last second and then running at him again.

Behind David, Aidan was watching the dogs with wide brown eyes and his hands over his ears.

"What is wrong with this dog?" David shouted over the barking. "He's seriously demented or something!"

"He's not!" I shouted back. "Bowser is making him nervous!"

"Ha!" David said. "Bowser's not even doing anything! Your dog is a spaz. Forget Duke; you should call him Mr. Meanie-Weenie."

Aidan started laughing. "Mr. Meanie-Weenie!" he cried. "That's so funny!"

"It's not funny!" I said. "Shut up!" I was talking to David and Aidan, but part of me was talking to my dog, too. He would not stop barking at Bowser. I grabbed the dachshund and picked him up out of Bowser's way. That made him stop for a second, but when he looked down and saw that Bowser was still glaring at him, he *rarf*ed a few more times.

"Charlie, honey, why don't you take him upstairs for a little while?" my mom suggested. She looked like she wanted to cover her ears, too.

"Fine," I said, although it wasn't fine at all because if you asked me, Bowser was the one being a big scary jerk, and *my* dog was just defending me. I knew how he felt. I wished I was brave enough to yell at David like that.

I stomped out of the kitchen carrying the dachshund.

"Can I come with you?" Aidan immediately asked, trailing behind us.

"No," I said. "I'm taking him to the attic."

"Oh," Aidan said. He stopped in the middle of the living room and watched me head upstairs with the dog. I wondered where Meowser was. She often hid when strangers came over, so I guess it made sense for her to hide from a new barking dog.

The attic is my place. A few years ago I asked my mom if I could go up there whenever I needed to get away from everyone else in the house. David has his own room, but I have to share with Aidan, so it only seemed fair. And Aidan was too little back then to climb the attic stairs by himself. He's big enough now, but he knows that he's not supposed to bother me when I'm in the attic. It's the one place I can go to get away from his questions and his constant poking about in my stuff.

Holding the dachshund under one arm, I pulled on the string that unfolds the attic stairs from the ceiling. It's pretty cool that I'm tall enough to reach it now; when I first started going up to the attic, I had to climb on a stool to do that. The trapdoor opened downward with a lot of creaking and moaning, and I pulled the stairs out the rest of the way.

Our house is really old, so it creaks and moans everywhere. All the wooden floors are warped in funny ways, so there are big gaps under some of the doors. When we first moved in, apparently there was fuzzy peach velvet wallpaper with glittery paisley patterns on it on all the walls. I don't remember that, but Mom kept a sample so I've seen it. It was pretty hideous. She and Dad spent several weekends stripping it all off.

She talks about doing other stuff to the house sometime, like renovating the bathrooms, but she's too busy, and we all think it's fine the way it is.

The attic has always been my favorite room. It's as big as a whole floor of the house, crammed with stuff, and it's exactly the kind of place you would expect to go through to get to Narnia. There's piles of old furniture up there, all dark wood and engraved bronze handles and funny lion's-claw feet. There's a huge old mirror with thick glossy copper vines woven around the outside. After I read the first Harry Potter book, I decided it was the Mirror of Erised and stared into it for hours, trying to make my strongest desire appear (although at the time I think my strongest desire was probably ice-cream sundaes, so it wouldn't have been very exciting).

The deal is that Mom lets me use the attic if I dust it and sweep it once a month for her. I know that sounds like it would be hard because there's so much stuff up there, but actually it's really fun because I'm always finding something weird that I've never seen before. All my grandparents' stuff on my dad's side ended up in our attic when they moved to Florida, so there are trunks of really old clothes and faded black-and-white photos and goofy old board games and mysterious devices which I guess did old-fashioned things that are now done by computers.

In the back corner, next to the big round window and under one of the skylights, I've cleared a space for my stuff. There's a large squishy denim beanbag, a pile of dark blue and green blankets, a small lamp, a portable electric heater, and a wooden crate full of my favorite books. I'm going to put my telescope here as soon as I've saved enough to afford one. Then I can sit here at night and look at Mars and think about how I'm going to go there one day.

It is by far the best spot in the house, mainly because no one can come up here but me, and only

Mom sometimes sticks her head through the trap-door opening to call me down for dinner. (She used to come up every time to check that I'd turned off the heater, too, but since I was really good about it, she trusts me to remember it myself now.)

I flung myself down on the beanbag and set the dog on the wooden floor. He'd calmed down a lot as we were climbing the stairs, and now it was like he'd totally forgotten about David and Bowser. His eyes were bright and curious as he started sniffing around. His tail went up and his nose went down and he set off into the attic like he was on a mission of exploration.

"Just don't fall down the stairs!" I called after him.

He wagged his tail at me and kept sniffing.

"I have to pick a name for you," I said. "What do you think? Duke?"

He didn't look up from his sniffing.

"Prince?" I tried. "Come here, Prince!"

The dog stuck his nose in the small space under a wardrobe and pawed at one of the dust bunnies. He was so low to the ground that he could practically crawl underneath it.

"Emperor!" I said. "Who's a good boy, Emperor?"

The dachshund didn't even look back at me. Plus "Emperor" felt really silly to say out loud.

I looked at my crate of books and thought for a moment. The Oz books were on the top, but "Wizard" seemed like a weird name, too. I pulled out *The Lion, the Witch and the Wardrobe* and flipped through it to the part about ruling Narnia.

"Of course!" I said. "I'm an idiot. Your name should be King! Because you're the king of any room you walk into, right?"

"Rarf!" the dachshund yelped. For a moment I thought he was agreeing with me, but when I looked up I realized he was barking at his reflection in the giant mirror. "Rrrrrr!" King growled. "Rarf!"

"Oh, stop," I said, getting up and going over to him. "That's just you, dopey."

"Rarf!" King said again. I didn't know if he really liked the name, but *I* liked it, so I figured I'd try it for a while.

"Come on, King," I said. "Come back over here." I tried to turn him around toward the beanbag, but he wriggled out of my hands and ran back at the mirror.

"Rarf rarf!" he yapped. "Rarf rarf rarf!" It seemed

to make him pretty mad that the dachshund in the mirror wasn't intimidated by him at all.

Luckily I knew the attic pretty well, so it didn't take me long to find an old sheet in a nearby trunk. I threw the sheet over the mirror and King blinked several times, as if that was an extremely baffling development. He looked up at me for a moment in confusion, and then shook himself and strutted back to the beanbag like, *That's right, I took care of THAT little problem. Out of my way, peons!*

I sat back down on the beanbag and took one of the treats Ruth had given me out of my pocket. "Here you go, King," I said. "Come here."

He took the treat delicately from my fingers, wolfed it down, and went over to investigate the pile of blankets. It wasn't really cold enough for the heater or the blankets yet, so they were still folded neatly . . . but not for long. King grabbed the top one between his teeth and dragged it to the floor, growling and shaking it.

"King!" I said, digging out another treat. "King, come!"

He shook the blanket a few more times for good measure and then dropped it on the floor and started *dig-dig-digg*ing at it with his front paws. He managed to pile it up into a little mountain, and then he dove at it and burrowed underneath. His butt and tail waved madly at me as he rooted around under the folds of green fabric.

"King," I said. "Seriously, buddy. What are you *doing*?"

He backed out of the blanket and shook himself all over. Lifting his chin regally, he finally decided to come back and let me give him a treat.

When I tried calling him without a treat in my hand, though, he completely ignored me. It wasn't because of his new name — he wouldn't come even when I used the name Milton and Ruth had been calling him, Chutzpah, or whatever that word was.

We didn't have long to practice anyway. Soon I heard Aidan calling me for lunch. I picked up King, checked to make sure I hadn't left anything on, and went back down the stairs. It takes two hands to lift the stairs and trapdoor back into place, so I put King on the floor of the hallway while I did that.

It only took ten seconds, but when I turned around again . . . he was gone.

CHAPTER 5

King?" I called. "King! Where are you?"

I looked down the stairs and saw Aidan at the bottom waiting for me. "Did King go down there?"

"King?" Aidan said, wrinkling his nose.

"My dog!" I said. "Obviously. Come on, Aidan. Did you see him?"

Aidan shook his head. "You really want to call him King instead of Yowser? Are you sure?"

"You're a lot of help," I said. I went to the door of my mom's room, but I couldn't see him in there. "King!" I called again. I crouched and looked under the bed.

"*RRRRRREEEEEOOOOOOOWW!!*"

A piercing yowl echoed down the hall. Meowser shot out of my room and bolted down the stairs in a blur of brown and black fur.

"Rarf rarf rarf rarf rarf!" King barked gleefully, galloping after her.

"Oh, no!" Aidan cried. "Meowser!"

I ran down the stairs after them. By the time I got to the kitchen, Aidan was standing on a chair holding Meowser in his arms. Meowser's fur was all fluffed out like she'd stuck her tail in a light socket. She was still going "Rreeooowwwrr! Rrreeoowrrr!" indignantly, showing her tiny pointed teeth as she meowed.

King was bouncing around the bottom of the chair, yapping at the top of his lungs. "RARF! RARF! RARF! RARF! RARF!"

The kitchen smelled of grilled cheese, but Mom and David and Bowser were all outside on the deck already. Aidan looked like he was about to cry.

"Help me!" he wailed as I came in. "Meowser is scared! I don't know what to do!"

"It's OK, don't freak out," I said. I ran over and picked up King. I held him tight even though he was wriggling in my arms like crazy and *rarf*ing like a lunatic. "See? It's fine. Meowser probably just startled him, that's all."

Mom pushed open the sliding door and came

inside. "What is going on in here?" she said. "I can hear the racket all the way at the other end of the garden."

"Charlie's dog was yelling at Meowser!" Aidan cried. Tears trembled in his eyes. "Meowser was so scared!"

"She's totally fine!" I said. She was, too. She'd stopped meowing and settled for glaring at King. Plus, by the way, she is a huge cat, totally bigger than King. She didn't have to be such a drama queen about it. "They were both startled! That's all that happened!"

Mom rubbed her forehead. "Charlie, could we maybe leave the dog in your room while we have lunch? Would that be all right?"

David smirked at me through the glass door. Bowser was sitting on the deck next to him, thumping his fat black tail on the boards and giving King the stink eye.

"It's not fair!" I said. "King didn't do anything wrong! He's just getting used to a new place. Why should he have to be punished?"

"It's not a punishment," Mom said. "It's just to give us a little peace and quiet until lunch is over.

Then you two can spend the afternoon in the yard with me while I garden. OK? Doesn't that sound like fun?"

"Fine," I said, stomping out of the kitchen with King in my arms. It wasn't fine and it wasn't fair at all and it was *my* birthday, but I knew if I tried to argue about it, things would just get worse. I set King inside our bedroom and told him to be good.

"I'll be back as soon as I can," I promised.

He wagged his tail until he saw me start to close the door, and then his head drooped and he looked confused.

"Sorry, King," I said. "I know it's not fair."

I closed the door on his woeful face and stomped back downstairs. Meowser was sitting on top of the fridge again, looking extremely displeased with the universe. She watched me through slitted eyes as I hauled open the sliding door and went out on the deck.

It was a pretty October day, sunny and really windy with clouds flashing across the sun and whirl-winds of yellow leaves swirling down onto the grass. I didn't want to spend my whole birthday being mad, so I tried to keep my mind on what it would be like to play outside with my very own dog.

None of us had much to say during lunch. Aidan asked me to pass the grapes and I managed not to throw them at him, which I thought was enough of an effort from me. Mom tried to ask David about his schoolwork, but David just grunted and mumbled something the way he always does. He finished first and stood up in a hurry. Bowser lunged to his paws behind him.

"David," my mom said in her warning voice.

"Can I be excused?" he said, but not very nicely.

She sighed. "Are you sure you and Bowser don't want to stay out here with me and Charlie? Maybe the dogs will get along better if they can play outside for a while. And you could use the fresh air."

"I'm busy," he said, hunching his shoulders and shoving his hands in his pockets.

Yeah, right. I'm sure he's *so* busy playing video games and lying on his bed staring at the ceiling blasting out his eardrums with terrible music or whatever.

Mom sighed again. (She does that a lot when she's talking to David.) "You're excused."

David and Bowser disappeared into the house. I crammed the last corner of my sandwich into my mouth. "Can I go get King?" I asked.

"No talking with your mouth full," Aidan scolded. I crossed my eyes at him and opened my mouth so he could see my half-chewed food. He giggled. "Gross!"

"Yes, all right," Mom said.

I put my plate and my glass in the dishwasher and ran upstairs. When I threw open my bedroom door, I saw King in the middle of the round tomato-red carpet between my bed and Aidan's. He sat up in a hurry, ducked his head, and gave me a guilty look.

"Uh-oh," I said. "What did you do?"

I took a step forward and realized he'd been chewing on something. I picked it up and saw it was one of Aidan's toy dinosaurs — the triceratops, if the half-eaten horns were any indication.

"Aw, man," I said. "King! Aidan's going to throw such a fit!" I looked around the room. With my luck, Aidan would come bursting in any minute. I did *not* want to fight about my dog again. Especially over a dumb toy that Aidan was too old to be playing with anyway. Usually he just set his plastic dinosaurs out on the rug and gave me lectures about their fighting styles, which I tried really hard to ignore while I did my homework.

It wasn't safe to hide the chewed-up toy in my

closet, because Aidan went in there all the time — remember, he has no idea what "privacy" is supposed to mean. And if I threw it under my bed, King would most likely drag it back out the moment he had time to chew on it again.

I ended up burying the dinosaur at the bottom of our hamper, under all our dirty clothes. I'd have to think of a better hiding place later, but at least Aidan wouldn't look for it there.

King sat in the middle of the rug with his head bowed, watching me with a worried expression.

"It's all right, King," I said. "You could have done something much worse, trust me." I crouched down and scratched behind his ears with both of my hands. "You're a good boy, don't worry about it. Come on, let's go outside!"

He jumped to his paws and shook himself all the way down his long hot-dog body. Then he lifted his head proudly and trotted ahead of me out the door and down the stairs to the kitchen. We saw no sign of Meowser as we went through, so I guess she heard us coming.

Aidan waved at me from the far side of the garden as we came outside. "Look what we're doing, Charlie!"

he called. He and Mom were kneeling on the grass beside one of the empty flower beds. Mom was poking around in the dirt with her banana-yellow gardening gloves on. Aidan had a stubby trowel in his right hand.

King sniffed around under the table on the deck, looking for crumbs from our sandwiches. I jumped down the three stairs to the yard and wandered over to Mom and Aidan.

"We're planting blubs!" Aidan cried. "They're going to be flowers! Daffodils and tulips and everything!"

"Bulbs," Mom corrected him, taking the trowel out of his hand and turning over some of the soft black earth with it. A box of weird white and green turnip-looking things was sitting next to her.

"What'd I say?" Aidan asked.

"Blubs," I answered, and he cracked up.

"Blubs! That's so funny!" I guess he was over the trauma of King chasing Meowser. Mom laughed, too. Aidan makes her laugh all the time.

King came bounding across the grass with his ears flying out behind him. For a dog with such short legs, he could run pretty fast. I jumped up and ran away and he chased me around and around the yard, barking happily. When I tripped and fell, he ran over and leaped on my chest so he could lick my face.

It was exactly what I always thought having a dog should be like. I felt like balloons of happiness were filling up inside my chest.

I should have known it wouldn't last.

CHAPTER 6

After about half an hour of chasing me around the yard and pouncing on fugitive leaves, King flung himself down in the grass and closed his eyes. His long ears flopped out on either side of his head and his stubby back legs stuck out straight behind him.

"Tired already?" I teased, but I was ready for a rest, too. I went inside to get my book and my sketch pad. By the time I got back outside, King was on his paws again. He was standing next to Mom and Aidan, watching them plant the bulbs in the ground. His nose quivered and he leaned forward like he was trying to figure out what they were burying. Aidan reached toward him to pat his head, but King jumped back and *rarf*ed at him.

"Come here, King!" I called.

He acted like he had no idea what I was saying. He didn't even look at me.

I went over and picked him up. It was awesome having a small dog that I could pick up whenever I wanted. That was one of the reasons I'd chosen a dachshund. If I'd gotten a dog the size of Bowser, I would have had to grab his leash and wrestle him wherever I wanted him to go. But with a little dog like King, I could easily pick him up to get his attention or stop him from being bad or whatever.

He gave me a startled look when I picked him up, but when I rubbed his chest, he leaned back and licked my ear. I laughed and carried him over to our hammock.

"You could help us plant if you want to, Charlie," Aidan offered.

"No thanks," I said, climbing into the hammock. We all do chores around the house, but gardening is Mom's thing, and she never makes us help if we don't want to, so Aidan is the only one who ever does.

I settled King on my lap, hoping he'd fall asleep while I did my art class homework and read my book. I was a few chapters from the end of *Many Waters*, by Madeleine L'Engle, and I couldn't wait to see what was going to happen. Plus if I finished it, I could start one of the Roald Dahl books that I knew Mom was giving me for my birthday.

King wasn't interested in napping anymore. He climbed around on my legs and chest for a while until he found a position where he could stand on me and peer out of the hammock at Mom and Aidan. It meant I couldn't really use my pencil to draw, and I had to hold the book up at a weird angle so I could read it over his head, but at least he'd stopped moving, so it was OK. I don't know what he thought was so amazingly fascinating about gardening, though. It always looks dead boring to me.

I could hear Aidan exclaiming over each bulb. "And what color is *this* going to be?"

"The daffodils will be yellow or white," Mom said. "But the tulips will be lots of colors — dark red and indigo purple and hopefully bright orange, too, if I picked out the right ones."

Finally they finished planting the bulbs and went inside to get cleaned up. I finished my book a few minutes later and went after them. I told King to come with me, but he balked at the foot of the deck stairs and backed up, looking at the garden and then looking at me.

"You want to stay out here?" I said. "That's OK, if you want to. I'll be back in a minute."

"RARF!" King agreed. He turned and trotted back into the garden.

I wasn't worried about him out there. We have a really high fence all around the yard, so I knew he wasn't going anywhere. I went inside, put away my book, and washed my hands. I was about to go back outside when the phone rang.

"I'll get it!" I shouted as I picked up the cordless. "Hello?"

"Happy birthday to you! Happy birthday to you! Happy BIRTHDAY, dear CHARLIE! Happy birthday to you!" The two voices on the other end of the phone started laughing.

"Hey guys!" I said. Satoshi and Midori are in my class at school. We have two sets of twins — Emmy and Kerri Drake are the girl twins, and Satoshi and Midori are the boy-girl twins.

"Did you get the dog?" Midori asked breathlessly. She always sounds like she's in the middle of a marathon, because she is so hyper she pretty much never stops moving. I bet she was jumping around her bedroom while she talked on the phone.

"I did!" I said. "I decided to call him King. He's *awesome*. You guys should come over and meet him!"

Satoshi groaned. "We have our grandparents' anniversary dinner tonight," he said. "Mom is making us stay home all day to help cook and clean the house."

"Oh, right," I said. "I forgot about that."

"The whole place smells like fish," Midori added. "Fish and Windex. Blech."

"Maybe tomorrow after school?" Satoshi suggested hopefully.

"Yes!" Midori shouted. "Swim practice was canceled because half the team has the flu, so I'm free! Let's do it!"

"I'll check with my mom," I said, grinning. "But it sounds great to me! I'll call Arnold, too." My friends hardly ever come to my house. They always have excuses, but I think it's because they're a little afraid of David and Bowser. Not that I blame them. But it was exciting to have a really great reason for them to come over anyway.

"Cool," Satoshi said.

"Uh-oh, Mom is calling," said Midori. "Have a great birthday, Charlie! We'll see you tomorrow!"

They hung up in a hurry. I love their house because they have a million weird toys and games and gadgets and their parents are always supernice to me, but it does seem like Satoshi and Midori are constantly busy with chores or extra classes.

Mom came into the kitchen as I was about to dial Arnold's number. She had showered and changed into a coppery red dress that matched her hair. I asked her if my friends could come over after school on Monday, and of course she said yes, because she wouldn't even be there. It was Giovanni who'd have to deal with us. But he never minds Aidan's millions of friends coming over, or even David's grumpy-looking fellow eighth graders, so I knew he wouldn't mind Satoshi and Midori and Arnold either.

Arnold lives next door and he's the best athlete in our grade, although Satoshi is nearly as good at baseball and Midori can usually stop about half of his goals when we play soccer together — but she stops *all* the rest of our goals, so that's saying something! We don't let her play goalie anymore because it makes the game no fun when no one can score.

Arnold's younger brother, James, is in Aidan's class at school, so we see them a lot. I knew they were going to be so jealous that I finally had a dog.

But before I could get through dialing his number, Mom got to the screen door and made this weird half-scream, half-strangled noise, like "AAAAAUUCK!"

"What is it?" I said. "What happened?"

She pointed at the deck. Her mouth opened and closed like she didn't know what else to say.

I hung up the phone and hurried over.

Right outside the sliding door, arranged on the deck, was a neat line of dirt-covered bulbs, with a trail of black earth leading back down the steps into the garden.

And I bet you can guess who was sitting behind the bulbs, panting and wagging his tail like this was the proudest moment of his life.

CHAPTER 7

"Uh-oh," I said.

"UH-OH!" Mom shouted. "Look what he did to my garden!"

King's nose and paws were covered in telltale dirt. Back by the fence, I could see giant holes where the bulbs had all been neatly planted half an hour earlier.

"He was trying to help!" I said desperately. "He probably thought you wanted them back! I mean, look how he brought them to you. Aw, his tail is wagging. He thinks he did something good."

Mom clutched her hair. "My *garden*," she said again. I knew King and I were in big trouble. Mom's garden is her pride and joy. If she decided King couldn't be trusted near it, I was afraid he'd be back at the Schwartz foster home in nanoseconds.

"I'll replant them," I promised recklessly. "I'll do it right now, I swear, it'll be as good as new."

She looked at her watch. "I don't have time to

show you how," she said. "Not if I'm going to make it to the supermarket and the bakery and the dry cleaners while they're still open. And besides, I've just showered." She looked at the bulbs mournfully. "I guess next weekend won't be too late. . . ."

"I can show him how to plant them!" Aidan chirped from the kitchen doorway. "I did it perfectly, remember, Mom? That's what you said! Charlie and I can do it. Right, Charlie?"

What I really wanted to do was finish the sketch of the *Voyager* spacecraft that I was supposed to be drawing for my art class on Tuesday. Planting daffodils with my little brother was not exactly how I'd wanted to spend my birthday. But if it was the only way to save King, I couldn't exactly say no.

"Sure," I said. "We'll have it all done before you get home. I promise."

Mom thought about it for a long minute, but finally she said, "All right. But call me if you have any questions — I'll have my BlackBerry. And from now on, keep an eye on that dog!"

"I will," I said, shooting King a stern look. He thumped his tail on the deck, still looking way too proud of himself.

"Yay!" Aidan cheered. He grabbed Mom's gardening kit from its hook by the door. His smile was ridiculously big as he followed me outside. King jumped up and pawed at my legs and got dirt all over my jeans. He looked like he was saying, *Did you see what I did? All by myself? Isn't that amazing?*

"You are in so much trouble, King," I said. But I couldn't stay mad at his cute face. I scratched behind his ears with one hand and tried to brush dirt off his nose with the other, but he wriggled away from me and bounded into the yard.

Aidan and I gathered up the bulbs on the porch and took them back to the patch of dark soil.

"Mom *bought* this dirt," Aidan said importantly. "It's better than all the other dirt. She uses it for the best flower beds."

I looked around the yard and realized there was darker earth all around the edges and under the flower bushes. I guess I'd probably seen her spreading dirt before, but I'd never thought about where it came from.

"That's weird," I said. "Buying dirt?"

Aidan giggled. "I think so, too!" he said. He knelt down and started using a trowel to fill in and smooth out the giant holes. "How many bulbs did he dig up?" he asked.

I counted the bulbs scattered on the grass beside us. "Eighteen," I said. I had to admit, I was a little impressed at how fast King had worked.

"That's half of what we planted," Aidan said, poking in the dirt with his fingers. "Look, I think he got them all up to here. The rest are still in place."

"Rarf!" King barked suddenly, pouncing on Aidan's hands out of nowhere. Aidan yelped and jumped back, and King immediately started digging in the dirt with wild fury.

"Stop!" I shouted. "King, NO! No digging! Stop!"

He paid no attention to me. His front paws paddled frantically and dirt flew out behind him.

"I said STOP!" I yelled, grabbing King and lifting him off the ground. His paws kept moving for a moment like a cartoon character who's just run off a cliff into thin air. Then he stopped and went floppy and twisted around to give me an outraged look.

"No digging," I said firmly.

He blinked, and his expression was so similar to Aidan's when he's trying to look innocent that I started laughing. But I knew that the minute I put him down he'd try to start digging again.

"I'm going to tie him to the deck rail," I told Aidan.

"Poor Yow — uh, King," Aidan said.

That annoyed me all over again, and not just because he nearly got my dog's name wrong. He didn't have to feel sorry for King, as if they were friends and I was the big mean punishing one. I frowned and carried King over to the deck. His leash was just inside the kitchen, and it was easy to wrap it around one of the railings before clipping it to his collar. He could still jump around on the grass, but there was nothing interesting to dig up over here.

King made a sad whining noise as I walked away and he realized he couldn't follow.

"Don't worry," I said. "We'll be right over here."

He lay down and rested his chin on his paws, watching me closely.

It turned out planting bulbs wasn't that hard at all, especially since the dirt was really easy to dig in. They only needed to be a few inches deep in the ground and pointing in the right direction, I guess so the daffodils wouldn't grow straight down instead of up.

I'd expected Aidan to act like a little know-it-all about it, but after he showed me what to do, he asked me about the book I was reading, and so we spent the rest of the time talking about *Many Waters* and how he really ought to read *A Wrinkle in Time*.

By the time we were almost done, I wasn't annoyed with him anymore. So of course that's when David had to show up and ruin everything.

CHAPTER 8

King warned us by barking like a maniac. "RARF RARF RARF RARF RARF RARF!" he hollered, straining on the end of his leash and flailing his stubby front legs in the air. I turned around and saw the sliding door open. Bowser came lumbering outside and stopped at the top of the deck stairs, glaring down at King.

David followed, shutting the door behind him. "Shut *up*, dog!" he shouted at King.

"RARF RARF RARF RARF RARF!" King shouted back.

"SHUT UP!" David roared. His black T-shirt was rumpled and his hair was mussed as if he'd been sleeping, which is entirely possible, since I have no idea what else he's doing in his room all the time.

"Stop bothering him and he will!" I yelled.

David went just close enough to King so that the dachshund couldn't reach him and made a horrible face at my dog. King stopped barking in surprise and sat down to stare at him.

Laughing nastily, David came across the yard to us with Bowser at his heels. Bowser growled at the trowel Aidan was holding and David raised his eyebrows.

"What are you girls doing?" David asked. "Getting ready for a meeting of the Ladies' Gardening Club? Shouldn't you be wearing frilly aprons and sun hats?"

"Gardening isn't just for girls," Aidan said, bristling. "I've seen lots of big guys in trucks that say 'gardener' on the side!"

"Right, and I bet they all love planting delicate little daffodils," David said.

"That's funny," I said. "If you're such a tough guy, isn't it kind of odd that you recognized the bulbs right away?"

David's neck turned red like it does when he's mad. Aidan gave me an admiring look.

"If you're not careful," David said, "someone's going to mistake Mr. Meanie-Weenie for a hot dog and eat him. And good riddance!"

King decided to add his two cents. "RARF RARF RARF!"

"His name is King!" I said hotly.

"I bet he'd be good with ketchup and relish," David said, licking his lips. "Right, Bowser? Who wants a Mr. Meanie-Weenie for dinner?" Bowser wagged his tail at David as if they weren't having a totally malicious, gross conversation.

"RARF RARF RARF RARF RARF!"

"Don't talk about Charlie's dog that way," Aidan said.

David squinted at him. "And a kitty cat sundae for dessert! Mmmm, fried whiskers."

"Oh, please," I said, hoping Aidan wouldn't cry and make us both look like babies. "Bowser is too fat and lazy to eat either Meowser or King. Just like you're too fat and lazy to walk your own dog."

"I don't see him complaining," David said with a smirk. "Unlike Mr. Meanie-Weenie over there."

"RARF RARF RARF RARF RARF RARF RARF!"

"*King* is complaining about *you*, because you're a big *jerk*," I said. "Hey, what's all over your hands?"

"Nothing," David said, hiding them quickly behind his back. But I was sure I'd seen splotches of red and white on his hairy fingers. "Come on, Bowser, let's leave these losers and their yappy sausage frolicking in the daffodils."

He stomped off to another corner of the yard with Bowser close behind him, sniffing the air and casting dark looks at King.

"That's the last one," Aidan said, patting the dirt carefully with the trowel. He looked less cheerful than usual, but that's the effect David has on everyone.

"OK," I said, standing up and brushing dirt off my jeans. "I'm going in to shower." Aidan got up to follow me to the deck, and that's when I realized that Aidan had been wearing my favorite shirt the whole time he'd been gardening. It was *covered* in black earth and grass.

"Aw, man," I said. "Aidan, you couldn't change out of my shirt first? Look what you did to it."

"Oops," Aidan said. "Oh, no! I'm sorry, Charlie."

"Whatever," I said. I untied King and took him inside without saying anything else. I couldn't even look at Aidan in my dirty shirt.

"I really am sorry!" Aidan called after me as King and I ran up the stairs to my room.

I didn't bother answering him.

For dinner Mom brought home my favorite Indian food and a birthday cake from the bakery. Arnold and James came over from next door to join us.

"RARF RARF RARF!" King announced as they came in the door. He backed up, staring at them and barking. "RARF RARF! RARF!"

"Oh, cool!" said Arnold.

"He's so cute!" said James. "Can he do tricks?"

"Uh — not yet," I said. "We're going to work on that."

"Fat chance," said David. "Look at the size of his head. Imagine what a tiny little pea brain he must have to fit in there."

"It's not always about how big you are," Aidan said importantly. "Stegosaurus was a huge dinosaur, but he had a brain the size of a walnut."

"Sounds like you, David," I said, and Arnold cracked up.

"Ha ha ha," David said meanly. "Mom, can I go upstairs yet?"

"Not until after dinner," Mom said.

"Rarf rarf rarf rarf rarf rarf!" King barked, spotting Meowser as she jumped onto the top of the fridge. He ran over and tried to jump up the fridge door, scrabbling at it with his front paws. His ears flopped back so you could see the pale pink undersides. "RARF RARF RARF RARF!"

"Sweetie, could we put King upstairs while we

eat dinner?" Mom asked me, rubbing her forehead. "Otherwise I'm afraid none of us will get a word in edgewise."

"But Arnold came over to meet him!" I said.

"You can bring him back down after dinner. All right?" Mom said.

"Fine." When Mom wasn't looking, I stuck out my tongue at Meowser. She lashed her tail and blinked her dark amber eyes at me.

David smirked as I carried King upstairs, still barking. This time I checked our bedroom floor carefully to make sure there was nothing for him to chew on. I piled Aidan's plastic dinosaurs on a shelf out of King's reach and threw everything else inside our closets. He flopped down on the rug with a sigh like he was ready for a nap anyway.

I opened my birthday presents before dinner. Mom had given me exactly the books I'd asked for, plus a couple on dog training that looked interesting, too. Of course King was my big present for the year, which was OK by me.

She always gives each of us twenty dollars to spend on a present for our brothers, so Aidan got me a new soccer ball and a jigsaw puzzle of the Mars Rover with the landscape of Mars in the background. David gave me a twenty-dollar bill in an envelope, but that was an improvement on the two-dollar keychain he tried to give me last Christmas, so Mom just raised her eyebrows and shook her head.

Arnold got me a new book by Kenneth Oppel and a board game called Cranium. It was cool having Arnold and James there to sing "Happy Birthday" over the cake with us, especially since I usually have a whole big party. But I didn't mind not having one this year — it was worth it to have King instead.

At least, I was pretty sure it was worth it. Although from the way the rest of my family looked at him, I knew I had a long way to go before they agreed with me.

CHAPTER 9

The rest of the evening was kind of a disaster. Arnold and James stayed to watch my favorite movie with us — *Toy Story*, which even has a dachshund (kind of!) in it! — but we had to turn it off halfway through because *somebody* kept barking every time he saw Meowser, or if Aidan or James tried to pet him, or if I shifted on the couch too suddenly and woke him up. Plus David kept walking through the room with Bowser, which really sent King into a frenzy, so I'm sure David was doing it on purpose.

King also decided for some reason that the couch must have something interesting buried in it, because he kept diving at the cushions and *dig-dig-dig*ging with his little paws until he'd knocked them onto the floor. Or if he couldn't knock them off because we were sitting on them, he tried to burrow down behind our backs and got stuck between the cushion and the back of the sofa. Arnold and I were the only ones who thought it was funny to see King's little butt sticking out with his back legs scrabbling frantically. After we had to pause the movie and rescue him for the tenth time, Mom suggested that it might be time to call it a night.

Arnold and James went home and Mom went to bed early with a headache. I set up King's dog pillow on the floor next to my bed and read for a while after Aidan went to sleep. To my relief, King fell asleep right away. He didn't even wake up when Meowser snuck in and curled up on Aidan's feet like she usually does. I guess he'd had a tiring day of nonstop barking and digging and fending off strangers.

He looked really cute with his long silky ears flopping over the edge of the pillow. His little legs kept twitching in his sleep, as if he was dreaming of chasing me around the yard. He was so long and sleek and handsome and friendly — nothing like scruffy, grouchy Bowser or standoffish, suspicious Meowser.

If only he could be quiet and good as well, he'd fit into this family just fine.

I don't know if I dreamed about playing with King, because I was woken up very abruptly on Monday morning.

"RARF RARF RARF RARF RARF RARF RARF!" he bellowed, shocking me and Aidan awake. I sat up, blinking and confused. It took me a moment to figure out that he was barking at Meowser; he'd finally woken up and noticed her in the room. Her fur bristled as she glared down at him from Aidan's bed.

Our bedroom door opened and Giovanni stuck his head in.

"Wow," he said. "I was about to wake you, but I guess someone took care of that for me." He grinned at King.

"RARF RARF RARF RARF RARF!" King shouted even louder. He looked very alarmed by this new person suddenly appearing in the doorway.

"King, shush!" I said. "That's just Giovanni! He's all right!"

"RARF RARF RARF!" King protested, like, *But I don't know him! And he's tall! And where did he come from? And this is all very alarming! And I think you should get up and do something about it! Now! Right now!*

"I'm sure we'll get used to each other today," Giovanni said, looking over his wire-framed glasses at King. "Right, little guy?" He tapped his watch, raising his voice to be heard over the barking. "Half an hour, guys."

Aidan and I got up and got dressed, and then I carried King downstairs to let him out. Giovanni gave me a banana to eat while I took King outside. I knew he couldn't be trusted out there alone with those bulbs. He sauntered around, sniffing and pawing at the dirt, but I managed to steer him away from the daffodils, and when we came back in, the garden was still intact.

I warned Giovanni about King's digging problems while we ate breakfast. As usual, Mom had left for work at the crack of dawn. She does something involving money and law and computers and briefcases. Apparently she's very important in the company; her BlackBerry is always beeping and she's the boss of, like, four hundred people or something ridiculous. She works crazy hours during the week, but then she doesn't have to work on the weekend, so we get her all to ourselves then.

Giovanni has been taking care of us for the last four years. He's working on a sociology degree, but I think if he could hang out with us as his job for the rest of his life, he'd be OK with that. He has curly dark brown hair and a big round face and a huge smile and he loves playing soccer with us, although he says his parents and the rest of his family in Italy would call it "football."

King was definitely not sure about him. The dachshund kept sidling behind me whenever Giovanni came near us, and when Giovanni walked away again, he'd pop his head out and *rarf!*

He also did his crazy *rarf rarf*ing thing when David thundered through the kitchen with Bowser, grabbed a Pop-Tart, and thundered out again. Giovanni has given up on trying to feed David a healthy breakfast. In fact, we all know better than to even try talking to David first thing in the morning, because he might just bite your head off. It's safer to stay out of the way until the door slams behind him and he's running up the block to catch his bus.

Bowser always sits by the door for a while after David leaves. He's the only one who's ever sad that David's gone. His tail wags when David pats him good-bye, and then it slows down as David goes out the door, and then his whole body droops when the door closes. He waits on the welcome mat for a few minutes, and then he sighs heavily and slowly heaves himself upstairs to spend the day waiting on

David's bed. Giovanni lets him out around midday, so he was going to do that for King, too.

"Be good," I said to King as we headed out the door. "No barking at Giovanni!"

The dachshund tilted his head at me curiously. His left ear nearly brushed the floor when he did that, and his eyes shone like bright polished marbles. I wished I could stay home and play with him instead of going to school.

The day went by *so slowly*, I swear it was like someone had frozen time. At lunch, Midori brought Michelle Matiba over to sit with us again. Michelle is cool, but it was still kind of weird to see her not sitting with Rosie Sanchez and Pippa Browning. I guess they were in a fight or something; Rosie kept twisting around to stare at our table. Midori normally hung out with Satoshi and Arnold and me instead of with other girls, but she could have picked a much more annoying girl to be friends with, so we didn't mind Michelle.

Today Michelle was wearing a sky-blue scarf around her hair with patterns of flying white cranes on it. It was the same color as Midori's long-sleeved shirt and the twisty baubles holding up Midori's two long dark pigtails. I wondered if they'd planned to match like that.

Satoshi and Midori are always really careful to wear non-matching colors — if she wears light blue, he wears dark red, or if she wears pink he wears a really bright orange that clashes with it completely. I'm not sure why, since they get along so well — the other twins in our class, Emmy and Kerri, dress alike all the time but fight constantly.

"How's Tombo?" I asked Michelle. Her family had just gotten a new boxer, and from the stories she'd been telling us, he'd been kind of crazy to deal with at first.

She beamed at me. "He's awesome. He's madly in love with Chihiro." Chihiro is Midori and Satoshi's dog — she's a Weimaraner, which is a big beautiful dog who's this eerie cool silver-gray color. I was a little worried about introducing Chihiro to King . . . I had a feeling there'd be a lot of barking involved there. Luckily only Midori and Satoshi were coming to my house that afternoon. Chihiro never comes with them. She and Bowser were pretty growly with each other the one time they met.

Arnold had some sports thing so he couldn't join us, which meant it was just Satoshi and Midori climbing into Giovanni's car with me and Aidan after school.

"Hi Giovanni!" Satoshi and Midori chorused.

"Hey there," Giovanni said. He looked a bit more frazzled than usual as he pulled out of the parking lot. "Uh, Charlie, you might want to let King out as soon as you get home. He wouldn't let me anywhere near him today. He hid under your bed and barked at me whenever I went up to your room."

"Really?" Midori said. "But all dogs love you, Giovanni!" She was basing this theory entirely on Bowser and Chihiro, but I was pretty surprised, too. I thought Giovanni would be the one person King got along with besides me.

"King!" I called as we went in the front door. "King! I'm home!"

Meowser rushed over and purred at Aidan, rubbing her head against his knees like she always does. I could see Bowser slumped at the top of the stairs, which meant David wasn't home yet.

"King!" I called again. No response. "He doesn't really know his new name yet," I explained to my friends.

Bowser suddenly surged to his paws and came charging down the stairs. We jumped out of his way right before the front door flew open and David stomped in with his friend Harper. Bowser flung himself at David, slobbering with joy and wagging his tail so hard he nearly fell over.

This is always a weird moment to watch, because it's the one minute of the day when David actually smiles. He knelt down and rubbed Bowser's head and back while Bowser licked his ears.

"Hey Harper," I said nervously. She pushed the hood of her black sweatshirt back a little bit and nodded at me and Aidan, but didn't say anything.

I used to have kind of a crush on Harper. She's been best friends with David practically their whole lives — don't ask me why, because I think she's way too cool for him. She used to smile at me and talk to me about TV or music while she was waiting for David, but she's been weird ever since they started middle school. Now she wears a lot of dark makeup around her eyes and hunches her shoulders and doesn't talk. And I'm pretty sure she cuts her own hair, because it's a lopsided pale blond mess and much too short.

"Don't bug my friends," David snapped at me. He spotted Midori and Satoshi behind me. "Oh, great. More brats. Now this day is perfect."

"David, be cool," Giovanni said in a no-nonsense voice.

David rolled his eyes and grabbed Bowser's green leash from its hook by the door. "Come on, Harper," he said. "Let's take Bowser for a walk."

Harper shrugged. Bowser looked nearly ready to die of happiness as David clipped his leash on. They vanished out the door, and I could feel Midori and Satoshi breathing matching sighs of relief behind me.

"David and Bowser walking?" Giovanni joked. "I thought I'd never see the day."

"I'm surprised he even knew where the leash was," I said, and Midori laughed. Actually, I wondered if David was remembering what I'd said yesterday, about him being too fat and lazy to walk his own dog. He'd never admit it — but was that why he'd suddenly decided to walk Bowser?

"Nobody get me in trouble for this," Giovanni said, "but who wants leftover birthday cake?"

"Me!" Satoshi and Midori and Aidan all yelled at once.

"King!" I called again. When nothing happened, I said, "Maybe he's asleep. I'll go get him."

"We'll be in the kitchen," Satoshi said.

"With the cake!" Midori added, clapping her hands delightedly.

I hurried upstairs. The door to David's room was open a little so Bowser could wander in and out all day, and as I went by I could see a huge mess stretching from one wall to the other. Mom's room, on the other hand, was neat and perfect the way it always is, with all her shoes arranged on a shoe rack beside the closet so their toes lined up exactly.

"King?" I said, stepping into my room.

A small black nose poked out from under the bed.

"Hey silly," I said. "It's me! Remember me?"

King scrambled out from under the bed, shook himself, and strutted regally over to me so I could pet him hello. His tail started wagging as I scratched behind his ears and he ended up licking my hands and my face in a happy, wriggly way.

"Did you miss me?" I asked him. He wagged his tail in a way that I decided meant yes.

Right then I noticed something small and gray under my bed. My heart skipped a beat. For a moment I had a terrible feeling that King had gone into Mom's room and brought back her BlackBerry charger or something equally important and expensive.

But when I pulled it out, it was just a weirdly-shaped piece of plastic. It curved a bit and it had a few holes in it, and it didn't look like anything I'd ever seen before. It looked like it was supposed to belong to *something*, but I couldn't figure out what. At least it didn't have any teeth marks in it, so I guess King had decided it was worth saving, but not worth chewing on.

"What is this?" I asked King.

He wagged his tail and lifted his snout like he was saying, *I've been guarding that for you all day!*

"Well, thanks," I said, "but where did it come from?"

Wag, wag, wag. Unhelpful grin.

"OK," I said. "Bottom of the laundry hamper it is." I tucked it down next to Aidan's chewed-up dinosaur, hoping I could figure out what it was (and more important, *whose* it was) later, and then I carried King downstairs.

"Oh, he's amazing!" Midori cried as I brought him into the kitchen. "Look at his ears! Look at his paws! Look at his goofy little legs!" She pushed her half-eaten cake aside.

"He looks just like dachshunds in the movies!" Satoshi said, leaning over the table.

Midori laughed and laughed. "What did you think he would look like?" she teased. "Less glamorous, because the movie dachshunds wear all that makeup and have fashion consultants?"

"RARF RARF RARF!" King barked at them as I slid open the door to the deck. Midori and Satoshi jumped up to join me.

"Can I come, too?" Aidan asked, wiping a milk mustache off his face.

"No," I said. "We're doing older-kid things right now."

Aidan looked crestfallen, so I added, "Besides, I don't want to overwhelm King with people. He'll do better if there's not too many of us."

"It's OK, Aidan," Giovanni said. "You can help me figure out what to make for dinner."

Blech. With my luck, that meant asparagus, which was the one vegetable Aidan liked and I didn't. But it wasn't worth sticking around to argue about it. I slid the door shut behind Midori and Satoshi, led them down the steps, and set King on the grass.

He gave my friends a baffled look and ran off across the yard, barking. I loved watching him run. It was like a seesaw — his front half went down while his back half went up, and then his front half went up while his back half went down, up-down-up-down as he ran.

"Uh-oh," I said as King dove into one of my mom's flower beds. It wasn't the one with the bulbs, but I knew she wouldn't like him digging *anywhere* in her garden. I ran over and grabbed him, but he'd already managed to dig a hole big enough to stick his front end into.

He wriggled around and licked my face, scattering dirt all down the front of my dark blue shirt.

"I read about dachshunds last night online," Satoshi said as he and Midori caught up to me. "They were bred to chase badgers into their tunnels, so that's why he's so good at digging!"

"And burrowing," Midori said. "I saw one on TV that could disappear into a hole in the ground in, like, ten seconds!"

"Well, he's not allowed to dig and burrow out here," I said. "Seriously, King, Mom will kill us. She might even send you back to the Schwartzes if you don't behave."

"RARF RARF RARF!" King yapped over my shoulder at Satoshi and Midori.

"*And* you need to be nicer to my friends," I said to him. "Also Giovanni. Come on, King, chill out."

"RARF! RARF! RARF RARF!" He was wriggling around in my hands so much that I put him back on the ground. He shook himself all the way from his nose to his tail, barked one more time at Midori and Satoshi, and trotted off to do his business in the bushes.

"He's very cute," Midori offered, but I could tell she had her doubts about King, just like the rest of my family did.

"Yeah," Satoshi said skeptically. "Maybe he just needs a couple of days to calm down."

King poked his nose out of a hydrangea bush, saw that I was still standing with these nefarious strangers, and went "RARF!" in an outraged way before disappearing into the bush again.

I kicked the dirt back into the hole he'd left in the flower bed. I didn't want to admit how worried I was, but if I couldn't get help from my best friends, then who else could I ask? "To be honest, guys," I said, "I don't know what to do with him. He barks all the time, he doesn't like anyone but me, he wants to dig up my mom's garden, and according to the Schwartzes, he's totally untrainable. I thought getting a dog was a great idea ... but now I'm afraid it's more like a disaster!"

Satoshi immediately looked interested. He loves solving problems, especially if it involves building something. "Maybe we could make a barricade around your mom's flowers," he said. "I bet we could build a little fence or something to keep him out of the flower beds."

I shook my head. "Mom wouldn't like that. She's really particular about how the garden looks — little fences wouldn't exactly fit into her plan."

"The other thing you can do is tire him out," Midori said, sitting down on the grass so she could see King better. "Dogs who get lots of exercise are much better behaved than bored, restless dogs."

Satoshi rolled his eyes. "Thank you, Miss Animal Planet."

"Well, it's true!" she said. "That's why Dad and I take Chihiro on such a long walk after dinner every night! She loves it, and then she's really good and quiet for the rest of the evening."

"So that's all I have to do?" I said. "Walk him a lot?" I knelt down to check on what King was doing. I could see his fat little paws trotting around between the bushes and the fence, so at least I knew he wasn't digging. "What about in the winter?" I asked. "With short legs like that, he's going to have a tough time in the snow around here."

"There must be indoor stuff you could do with him, too," Midori said. "Oh! We should make up a game that's like badger hunting! That way it'll use his natural instincts, and he'll get out all that digging and burrowing energy."

Satoshi snorted and joined us on the ground. "What's a game that's like badger hunting? You want him to chase Meowser around the house?" He stopped and got that look on his face that means he's about to have a great idea.

"Aidan would have a heart attack if we let King chase Meowser," I warned.

"But we don't have to!" Satoshi said, snapping his fingers excitedly. "We can play hide-and-seek with King instead!"

I laughed. "I don't exactly see King standing in a corner and counting to twenty while we hide."

"Wait, Satoshi's right," Midori said. Her eyes were lit up like her brother's. "One of us can hold him while the other two hide treats or toys, and then we make him look for them. It's close enough to hunting. I bet he'll love it!"

For a moment I was excited about the idea, but then my spirits fell again. "Except it's not going to work if he won't go anywhere near you guys."

"Well, so that's step one," Midori said, jumping to her feet. "Come on, Charlie! This'll be such a fun project!"

"First things first," Satoshi said. "We need to get Giovanni to take us to the pet store."

CHAPTER 10

I'd only been inside Furry Tails, the town pet store, once, on the day before my birthday, when we went in to buy some stuff for King. Normally when Mom or Giovanni went in to get food for Bowser or Meowser, I would wait in the car, because it was too weird to look at all the stuff I wanted to get but couldn't because I didn't have a dog of my own.

But on Saturday I'd finally been able to choose all the dog stuff I'd wanted — a bright red leash and matching collar with a pattern of gold thread woven through it; a big white, squishy dog pillow with black dog bones all over it; the two little red dishes for his food and water; and a tiny red harness seat belt for the car.

We hadn't gone into the food aisle because we already had a giant bag of dog food for Bowser at home, and Mom said we could just use that for King as well. So I'd forgotten to get treats, and even worse (if you asked me), I'd also forgotten to get any toys for him.

Aidan trailed after us as we headed into Furry Tails. Giovanni insisted that we couldn't leave him at home alone, and David still wasn't back with Harper.

"Hey Aidan," I said, "why don't you go look at the hamsters while we check out the dog toys?"

Aidan glanced in the direction of the small rodent section. I knew he liked watching the mice and guinea pigs and gerbils playing on their wheels, so I was hoping he'd leave us alone for a while.

No such luck. "Can't I come pick a dog toy with you?" Aidan said. "There are so many good ones! Some of them squeak! I can help you find the perfect one!"

"Oh, he can come," Midori said. "He's no bother." She smiled at Aidan and he gave her a worshipful look.

"Fine," I said. "But I get to make the final decision, so no making a fuss about it."

"I never make a fuss!" Aidan said indignantly.

I was actually less worried about Aidan and more

worried about King. It was fun to bring him into the pet store with us, but what if he saw another dog and started barking?

Almost as soon as I'd thought that, we turned into the treats aisle and spotted a tiny, shaggy white poodle a few feet ahead of us.

"RARF RARF RARF RARF!" King bellowed, bracing his paws and looking up at me for backup.

The poodle jumped in surprise and spun around. When she saw King, her tail started wagging about a million miles an hour. She came bounding over toward him, yanking the pink leash out of her owner's hand.

"Uh-oh," Midori said under her breath as she saw who was on the other end of the leash.

"Buttons!" Rosie Sanchez yelped, stamping her foot. "Buttons, no! Get back here!"

Buttons paid no attention to Rosie; she was too excited about saying hello to King. She bounced into a play bow in front of his face with her little pom-pom tail wagging frantically. Alarmed, King retreated behind my legs. "Rarf?" he said, and to me it sounded like, *But I was so loud and scary! Why is she saying hi to me? I don't understand! Girls are weird!*

"Hi Rosie," I said.

"Hi Charlie," she said. "Hi Satoshi. Hi Aidan." She pointedly didn't say hi to Midori, but Midori was pretending to read the label on a package of treats as if she hadn't even noticed Rosie was there. Aidan looked from Rosie to Midori, his forehead wrinkled in confusion. He's still too young to understand how mysterious girls can be.

King poked his nose out to look at Buttons again. Buttons's tail wagged even harder. Slowly King took a few steps forward and sniffed her ears, then another step to sniff the rest of her. Buttons stayed still for a moment while he did that, and then suddenly she spun around and bounced on his head with a gleeful expression.

"Rarf!" King protested, but he only jumped back half a step.

"Ruff!" Buttons agreed and jumped after him. This time King dropped onto his back and flipped her over him. I let go of his leash so they could play. Soon they were both rolling around in the aisle, spinning and wriggling and *rrruff*ing and *RARF*ing. Aidan clapped his hands in delight.

"Awww," Rosie said, putting her hands on her hips. "That's adorable. Is that your dog, Charlie?"

"Yup," I said. "His name is King."

Rosie shot a look at Midori. "Isn't it *so* nice to have a *small* dog?"

Midori lifted her chin a bit higher and kept reading the treat label, although I could tell she was really watching Buttons and King out of the corner of her eye.

"Well, it works for me," I said. "But big dogs are nice, too."

"Like that one," Satoshi said, pointing. A golden retriever was sauntering past the far end of the aisle, sniffing the chew bones curiously. I recognized the dog from a couple of times when he showed up at school at the beginning of September. The guy holding his leash was Parker Green, and he was talking to Rosie's brother Danny as they picked out a big box of dog biscuits.

"Oh, *Merlin*," Rosie said, shaking her head and wagging her hands in the air. "Perfect, *amaaaazing* Merlin. Yeah, he's all right, if you don't mind finding fur all over everything."

"I'm going to check out the toy aisle," Midori said, putting down the treats. "Come on, Aidan. We'll see you guys there." She grabbed Aidan's hand and hurried him away without looking at Rosie.

I wanted to let King and Buttons play all day, but I knew we had to get going soon. Plus it felt kind of weird to be caught in the middle of Rosie and Midori's fight, whatever that was all about.

"Let's take these," I said, grabbing a big bag of small, chewy treats. The label said ALL NATURAL and REAL BEEF! so I figured King would like that. "See you around, Rosie."

"That was so cute — we should let them play again," she said, catching Buttons and picking her up in her arms. Buttons wrapped her paws around Rosie's neck and licked her cheek a couple of times until Rosie giggled. King sat on the floor and gazed up at Buttons in bewilderment. He didn't move as I picked up the end of his leash.

"Yeah, maybe," I said, although I could see Satoshi making a *No! Run while you can!* face behind Rosie's back.

"We go to the park all the time," she said. "Maybe we'll see you at the dog run."

"Sure," I said. "Yeah. Maybe."

"'Bye Charlie," she said with a big smile. "'Bye King! 'Bye Satoshi." She ran to catch up with Parker and Danny, her black curls bouncing.

"She's not that bad," I said to Satoshi when she was out of earshot. "She can be really nice. And she's great at math." We'd shared a table for the bake sale and she'd taken care of all the money stuff and acted really friendly.

"She's just crazy," Satoshi said, shaking his head. "A little too bossy for me. But I have to be on Midori's side anyway; that's the rule."

"What are they fighting about?" I asked as we headed for the toy aisle. "Do you know?"

Satoshi shrugged. "It's really Michelle who's fighting with her. Midori's not into all that drama, but she kind of got sucked into it when she made friends with Michelle."

"Girls," I said.

"Tell me about it," he said.

"Charlie, look what we found!" Aidan called, waving a couple of toys at me from the other end of the aisle, where he was standing with Midori. "These even look like badgers!" King's ears perked up when he spotted the toys.

"I explained about the badger hunting," Midori said with a grin as we came up. "They don't have any badger toys, but they do have a zebra, a panda, and a black-and-white cat."

"Or there are all of these," Aidan said rapturously. He gestured at the long row of toys. "Blue hippos! Green squeaky bones! Look, this one's a really fat duck!" He poked the shockingly yellow toy and it went "SQUUACK!"

"I like the zebra," I said, taking it out of Midori's hand. "What do you think, King?" I held it out and he tried to grab it from me.

"That seems like a good sign!" Midori said with a laugh as King tried to jump and climb up my leg to get to the zebra.

Aidan laughed, too, but then his eyes strayed back to all the other choices. "Could we get him more than one?" he asked.

"Let's start with one and see how he likes it," I said. "This is coming out of my allowance, after all." I've been saving my allowance for ages because I want to buy myself a telescope, although I haven't told too many people about that plan yet. But I knew I'd have to spend some of my saved-up money on King . . . I was just hoping to have a bit left over!

Aidan's face brightened. "I have an allowance, too!" he said. "I can buy King another toy with *my* money!"

"You don't have to do that," I said, frowning. I

didn't want to look like the bad guy who wouldn't spend money on his dog while my little brother lavished gifts on him.

"It's OK! I want to!" Aidan said. "Like a welcome-to-the-family present. Please can I, please?"

"Oh, why not?" Midori said. "I think it's a cute idea."

"I'm sure King won't mind an extra toy," Satoshi added.

As I've mentioned before, all my friends think Aidan is *so* cute.

"OK, fine," I said.

"Which one do you want?" Aidan asked. "You can still make the final decision." He beamed at me and I felt like a jerk.

"No, that's all right," I said. "You can pick."

"Really?" he said. He studied the toys with shining eyes as if this was the most important decision he'd ever had to make. "Well, if he has a zebra, he should get another jungle animal to be its buddy. Right? How about this one?" He pulled out an orange giraffe with purple spots and stubby purple horns on its head.

"Sure," I said with a shrug. King looked pretty interested in it. Interested enough that he wasn't avoiding Aidan the way he usually did. I wasn't sure I liked that.

"You guys all set?" Giovanni asked, strolling into our aisle. He was carrying a bag of kitty litter and a case of cat food tins.

"RARF! RARF!" King barked at him.

"Look what we got!" Aidan announced, holding up the giraffe and pointing at the zebra.

"Perfect," Giovanni said with a smile. "What a lucky dog."

Midori squeezed my elbow as we headed up to the cash register. "Ready?" she said. "Now we're going to discover all of King's hidden talents and teach him how to be a good dog! It's going to be so much fun!"

I nodded and smiled, but inside I was crossing my fingers and praying that she was right. If King had hidden talents, I definitely wanted to know about them. And if we could train him to be a good dog . . . well, I wasn't sure it would be fun, but it sure would be a miracle!

CHAPTER 11

We decided we had to start by making King like my friends. In the car to and from the pet store he sat on my lap and *rarf*ed grumpily at them over the back of the seat. When they tried to pet him, he lunged backward as if they were holding sharp, pointy weapons. I knew if we all wanted to play with him, he'd have to get used to them, and the sooner, the better.

"Don't worry," Midori reassured me. "Treats and toys should do the trick."

I told Aidan to go help Giovanni with dinner, and then the rest of us went up into the attic. Arnold thinks it's kind of spooky and haunted up there, but Satoshi and Midori love it as much as I do. I blocked off the trapdoor with a couple of trunks so that King wouldn't accidentally fall down the stairs, although I was pretty sure he was smarter than that.

"That's weird," I said, shoving the last trunk into place. "I thought this trunk was closer to the window last time I cleaned up here." I shoved it another inch. "And it feels lighter than usual, too."

"How can you keep track?" Satoshi asked, rubbing the polished wooden lid with his fingers.

"There's a system, it's just hard to explain," I said. "For instance, the stuff on that side is my grandparents' and the stuff over here, like this trunk, was my dad's."

"What are you reading now?" Midori asked, lifting books out of my crate. I told her about the books Mom had just given me. "Oooh," she said. "*The Witches* is great, but *Matilda* is my favorite."

"The one about a little girl who's a genius?" Satoshi said. "Gee, I wonder why you like that one."

"I'm not a *genius*," Midori said, but she totally is, and we all know it because Ms. Applebaum always gives her more advanced work to do so she won't get bored with the slow pace the rest of us have to learn at.

King pawed at the sheet over the mirror, as if he remembered finding a dog there the day before. I told my friends about that and they laughed.

"Chihiro did the same thing when she was a

puppy!" Satoshi said. "But she's used to mirrors now. She's like, 'Oh, it's you, boring mirror dog. Like, whatever.'"

"King, come here!" Midori called from the beanbag. King stuck his nose under a corner of the sheet and ignored her.

"At least he's not barking at us right now," Satoshi said.

"I'll get him," I said. I went over and showed them how to pick him up so it wouldn't hurt his back, the way Mrs. Schwartz had told me to, supporting his front end and rear end at the same time. King gave me a disgruntled look, like *Um, can't you see that I'm exploring here?*

"This'll be just as much fun, I promise," I said to him. I sat down on a blanket across from Midori and opened the bag of treats from the pet store.

That got his attention. King sat bolt upright and stared at the treat bag with his nose twitching. I took one out and let him gobble it off my hand.

"You like that?" I said. "Well, you can get more if you're nice to my friends." I tossed the treat bag to Satoshi, who sat down on the floor in kind of a triangle from me and Midori. He put a treat on his hand and held it out low to the ground.

King's eyes had stayed on the treat bag as it flew through the air over his head. He stared at the treat in Satoshi's hand, sniffing cautiously. With a couple of careful steps, he leaned off my lap and edged toward the outstretched hand.

"Don't move," Midori whispered. "Don't startle him."

Satoshi stayed perfectly still. King glanced up at his face, then looked back at me like, *Are you sure this is safe?*

I nodded encouragingly. "Good boy, King," I said. "Good boy. Take the treat."

The dachshund stretched himself as long as he could so his back paws were still touching my jeans. He reached his snout way, way out, and with a quick, darting motion, he slurped the treat off of Satoshi's hand and then ran back to me. Satoshi and Midori applauded.

"Good boy!" I said, scratching his sides. "What a good dog!"

"Now me!" Midori said. Satoshi handed her the treat bag and she did the same thing, putting the treat on her hand and resting it on the floor. "Here you go, boy," she said in a low voice. "Good King. Good dog."

King was still wary, but this time it didn't take him quite so long to go out and get the treat before running back to me. And as Satoshi and Midori passed the treats back and forth, he got more and more confident. Finally he even deigned to sit still in front of Midori long enough for her to pat his head while he ate his treat.

"Awesome!" Midori said. "Now if you do that with the rest of your family, he'll get used to them, too."

"That's OK," I said. "I kind of like that he likes me better than them."

"You may like it now," Satoshi said, "but just wait until you need someone else to walk him!"

"Let's try hide-and-seek!" Midori said, clapping her hands. "Charlie, you hold him here. Satoshi and I will go hide a couple of treats and the two toys somewhere in the attic. We'll see what he finds first!"

"Let him sniff the toys before we hide them," Satoshi suggested. I dug the toys out of the bag and held them up to King's nose. He seized the giraffe in his jaws and tried to wrestle it out of my grip.

"Nope, you have to find it first!" I said, laughing at the determined look on his face. I pried it loose and gave the toys to my friends. King watched them go off with his new giraffe in magnificent outrage.

"Don't look," I said, turning him toward the window. "No cheating."

"Hrrrrrruff," he huffed, but then a bird flew by the window and that distracted him from being furious with me.

"OK!" Midori called. "Time to seek!"

"Ready, King?" I said. I stood up and set him on the floor; he looked up at me with his tail wagging. "Ready — go find it!" I pointed out at the attic.

King looked in the direction I was pointing, then back up at me like, *Yes? And?*

"Go on!" I said. "Find it!"

He tilted his head in one direction, then the other.

"Maybe you should look with him," Satoshi suggested from his perch on a nearby armchair.

I started walking through the attic stuff as if I was searching for something. "Find it!" I said to King. "Where is it? Where could it be? Find it!" He padded along beside me, watching me intently. After a moment, it was like a lightbulb went off in his head. He started looking in the same direction as I was, sniffing the floor intently. When I turned, he turned, bouncing a few steps in front of me to scout ahead. I got down on all fours to peek under a blanket and he immediately burrowed all the way underneath it. He came back out shaking himself like, *Nope, nothing there, boss! Where should we look next?*

Midori giggled. "You're getting warmer," she said. "No, wait, colder. No, warmer! Nope, ice cold. It would help if you were crawling, of course."

"Why do I have a feeling you're laughing at me and not just at the dog?" I said.

"I would never!" she said innocently.

The first thing King found was one of the treats. It was sitting right on top of one of the bronze clawed feet of an old cabinet. He *rarf*ed with glee when he spotted it and pounced on it right away. In one chomp, it was gone.

"Good boy!" I cheered. "Hooray!"

"Long live the King!" Satoshi cried, laughing.

King found the other treat poking out of the key-hole of a leathery old trunk. A minute later, he spotted the zebra half-buried in the open bottom drawer of a chest of drawers. He dragged it out and shook it vigorously for a minute. Then he lay down on the floor and started chewing on one of its ears.

"There's still one more thing to find, dopey," I said.

Rrrumph rrumph rrrumph, went King, chewing and looking pleased with himself.

"OK," I said. "I think the zebra's dead. You killed it, you win. Now find the giraffe! Go on, King! Find it!"

It took a while, but either he got bored of the zebra or he realized I was still on the hunt and finally joined me. About ten minutes later, he found the giraffe at long last, propped on a cushion behind a stack of paintings. He came bounding over to me with it between his teeth, grinning like a maniac.

"Woo-hoo!" Satoshi whooped. King dropped the giraffe and then pounced on it as if it was trying to run away from him. He rolled around with it, tugging on its tail and making cute growling noises. It was hysterical.

When I finally stopped laughing and took it away from him, we played the game again with different hiding places, and this time he caught on a lot faster. It only took him fifteen minutes to have the zebra and the giraffe corralled back at the beanbag, where he sat on them with a very proud expression on his face.

"Who says you're untrainable?" I crowed. "You're the smartest dog ever!"

"Uh, Chihiro begs to differ," said Satoshi, but he was grinning, too.

I patted King's head and gave him another treat. "You're not a hot dog at all," I said. "You're a *hot-shot* dog."

Midori groaned. "Oh, you did not just say that."

King climbed onto my lap and I stroked his long, droopy ears. I felt a lot less worried than I had been since he'd arrived. "Yeah, OK," I said. "Maybe there's hope for you yet, buddy."

CHAPTER 12

Before Satoshi and Midori went home, I showed them the gray mystery thing King had hidden under the bed. I was careful to do it when Aidan wasn't around, just in case it was his. I hoped maybe they could help me figure it out so I could put it back wherever it came from before anyone noticed.

But they both shook their heads.

"Sorry," Satoshi said. "I have no idea what that is."

"Me neither," said Midori, turning it over in her hands. "Weird. Let us know when you find out, though!"

I left King upstairs while I walked my friends out. He was flopped on my rug looking exhausted, and he didn't even twitch when they both patted his head to say good-bye.

"You guys are magicians," I said as we went out

the front door. "It's so cool how all that actually worked! If only David would let you work that kind of magic on Bowser."

Midori shuddered. "That's OK," she said. "I'd love to save Bowser, but not if it means dealing with David."

"I can't believe he's still out," I said. We'd passed by his room and if he'd been in there, the door would have been closed. "It's been hours. How does Harper put up with him for that long?"

"Maybe they went to the park," Satoshi said. Their dad wasn't outside yet, so we sat on the front steps to wait. "We should take King and Chihiro to the dog run this weekend and see how they get along."

"Ooh, and Michelle can bring Tombo!" Midori said. "That would be fun!"

"If you guys made up with Rosie, she could bring Buttons, too," I said.

Midori was quiet for a minute, wrapping one of her pigtails around her finger. "Buttons is super-cute," she admitted. "Well. It'd be OK with me, but it's really up to Michelle."

Her dad's car pulled up before I could say anything else, but I hoped she would sort Rosie and Michelle out. I knew now that King would play with

Buttons — I wasn't sure how he'd react to Chihiro and Tombo.

"'Bye Charlie! See you tomorrow!" the twins yelled out the window as they drove off. I waved for a minute, and then in the distance up the block I spotted David and Harper coming back with Bowser trotting slowly between them. *Ruh-roh.* I didn't want to run into them if I could help it.

Quickly I scooted inside and ran upstairs.

"Where are you going, Charlie?" Aidan called from the kitchen. "Want to play outside with King? I finished my homework!"

"Maybe later," I called back.

King wasn't in the middle of the rug anymore. I glanced around the room, and then I crouched down and peered under the bed. Sure enough, he was curled in a little ball on the floor, snoozing away.

And nestled between his front paws was *another* mystery thing.

"King!" I said. "What did you do?"

He opened his eyes and blinked at me, all *Hey dude, I was sleeping here.*

I lay down on my stomach and pulled out the new object. It was silvery and metallic-looking and sort of cone-shaped, but with a rounded bottom instead of being pointy like an ice cream cone. It was a bit bigger than my hand. And again, it didn't look at all familiar.

"King, why are you so weird?" I said. "Where do you *get* this stuff?"

His tail thumped on the floorboards as if he were saying, *I know, I astonish even myself.*

The front door slammed, and almost at the same moment, Giovanni called, "OK! Time for dinner!"

I sighed and buried the silver cone thing at the bottom of the laundry hamper. King wrinkled his snout at me like he couldn't believe I kept taking his lovely stash of mystery things.

"Stay here and be good," I said. Just to be safe, I shut the bedroom door behind me.

David and Bowser were going into their room as I reached the top of the stairs. They both glared at me. "I hope you're leaving Mr. Meanie-Weenie up here," David growled. "We don't need him yapping away and giving everyone a headache during dinner."

"*Obviously* I'm leaving *King* up here," I said, spreading my empty hands. "I mean, do you see him?"

He snorted, went into his room, and slammed the door. I guessed that Harper had gone home.

Aidan was setting knives and forks on the table as I came into the kitchen. He looked up at me and smiled. "Guess what, Charlie?" he said. "Giovanni showed me how to make pizza dough! It's so cool! We put it in this machine and it goes round and round and round and you can watch it getting smushed and squished!"

"If we weren't lazy we'd use our hands instead of a machine," Giovanni said, adjusting his glasses. "But it should be OK anyway." He was slicing up a large round pizza covered in red and yellow peppers, ricotta cheese, and mushrooms.

"It smells awesome," I said. I got myself a glass of water from the fridge, ignoring the icy stare from the cat overhead.

"What did you guys do?" Aidan asked. "Did you play with the giraffe? Did King like the giraffe? Did you pick a name for it?"

"Yeah, he loved it," I said. "He's all worn out now —"

An enormous bang from upstairs cut me off. We all stood very still, even Giovanni, listening to David's angry footsteps thundering down the stairs.

"That doesn't sound good," Aidan whispered.

David burst into the kitchen. His neck and face were bright red with fury.

"Who's been in my room?" he demanded. "Who's been touching my stuff? Which one of you was it?" He narrowed his eyes at Aidan and then at me.

"It wasn't me!" Aidan said quickly. "I've been down here with Giovanni all day!"

"Me neither!" I said. "Satoshi and Midori and I were in the attic with King! We haven't gone anywhere near your room!"

"You're lying!" he yelled. "Somebody went into my room and snooped around and took my stuff! I want it back!"

Uh-oh, I thought. Was that where King had gotten the gray piece and the silver cone? But why would David be so upset about a couple of weird little things? It wasn't like King had run off with his PlayStation controller or something. And how had he even noticed such small things were missing in the big mess of his room?

Well, I definitely didn't want to admit to something that I wasn't sure I'd done, especially when it would only get King in more trouble with my family.

"What, uh — what exactly are you missing?" I asked.

David huffed for a second. "That's none of your business," he snarled.

"David," Giovanni said reasonably, "if we don't know what's missing, how can we help you find it?"

"The person who took it knows what he took!" David shouted. "Just give it back!" He took a threatening step toward me.

Giovanni jumped in his way, making soothing motions with his hands as if he were taming a wild mountain lion.

"Shouting isn't going to solve this problem," he said. "Let's sit down over dinner and see if we can figure out what happened. OK?"

"I know what happened," David said. He jabbed a thick finger at me and then at Aidan. "My annoying little brothers did something annoying, nosy, and stupid. Again. I *will* find out who did this!" He whirled around and stomped out of the kitchen.

Giovanni sighed. "I guess I'll save him some pizza for later, then." He went back to the counter and divided the pizza onto five plates, setting two aside for Mom and David.

My mind was whirling. If those pieces were David's, I had to put them back without him knowing King had taken them. But if they weren't his, and he suddenly found them in his room, he'd be this mad all over again about one of us "snooping."

I glanced at Aidan. It didn't seem like him to go into David's room and take something. Maybe Giovanni had knocked something behind the desk when he went in to get David's laundry. Or maybe David had just misplaced whatever he was looking for. Maybe this wasn't King's fault at all.

I'd have to ask Satoshi and Midori for their advice at school tomorrow. Their parents didn't like anyone to call during dinner, and I always seemed to get it wrong when I tried to wait until afterward.

"RARF RARF RARF RARF RARF RARF RARF RARF RARF RARF RARF RARF!"

King's bark suddenly echoed through the house. I'd never heard him sound so wild and frantic. I dropped my plate back on the counter and ran upstairs. I could hear Aidan and Giovanni running behind me.

David was in our room, pulling things off the shelves and tossing clothes out of the closet. From under the bed, King was barking madly at him. I was glad he was smart enough to stay out of range of David's heavy boots.

Bowser sat in the doorway, looking confused. He didn't even growl at us as we squeezed by into the room.

"Hey!" I shouted. "Quit it! You're making a mess!"

"That's mine!" Aidan shrieked as a plastic velociraptor flew across the room and bounced off the opposite wall. "Stop it, David, stop it!"

"Whatever you're looking for, we didn't take it!" I yelled. I focused very hard on not looking at the laundry hamper. David hadn't touched it yet. He yanked open our drawers and started rummaging under our pajamas.

"Rarf rarf rarf rarf rarf rarf rarf rarf rarf!" King added.

"OK, that's enough," Giovanni said. He stepped forward and firmly closed the drawer David had pulled open. "This is not adult behavior," he said to David.

"How am I supposed to act like an adult when I'm living with two snooping babies?" David demanded.

"Either talk to me about this sensibly," Giovanni said, "or go to your room and think about how else to solve this problem. In a way that doesn't involve violence or property damage, please."

David glared at him. Even King stopped barking, as if he wanted to see what would happen. For a moment I thought David might try to fight or yell some more, but then he stepped back, pointed at me and Aidan one more time, and stalked out of the room. Bowser slipped in behind him just before David slammed his bedroom door.

Giovanni sighed. "I'll help you guys clean this up after dinner, OK?"

"Thanks, Giovanni," Aidan said, poking a pile of his clothes with his foot. Giovanni put his hand on Aidan's shoulder and steered him toward the stairs.

"You were a good watchdog," I said to King. I crouched down and slid a couple of treats under the bed. I could hear his tail whacking the underside of my mattress as he scarfed them up.

I backed out of the room, giving the laundry hamper one last guilty look.

Had King stolen those things from David's room?

Why was David so upset about them?

Was this all my fault?

CHAPTER 13

When Mom got home, Giovanni told her what had happened, and they went into her office to talk about it in quiet voices. David didn't come out of his room for the rest of the evening, although after we all went to bed I'm pretty sure I heard him sneak downstairs to get that pizza.

I didn't have a chance to ask my friends for advice at school because all anyone wanted to talk about at lunch was the announcement that Miss Woodhull, one of the sixth-grade teachers, was going to direct the fall school play and we could all try out for it next week. Not that I cared — there was no way you could get me up on a stage performing for a whole audience full of people. But Michelle and Midori were super-excited, and even Satoshi and Arnold kept trying to guess what the play would be.

"If it's a musical, Ella should get the lead," Midori

said. "Remember? The girl with the beagle who won the talent show?"

"Yeah, totally!" said Michelle. "You know, unless Miss Woodhull wants to give the lead to me." She flipped her emerald green scarf back and flapped her eyelashes dramatically. Midori cracked up. Midori, by the way, was wearing an emerald green shirt and earrings, so I guess I was right about them planning to match.

I couldn't really concentrate on the play conversation because I was too worried about what King might be doing while I wasn't home. The worst part was that I wasn't even going straight home from school. I had my art class after school with Mrs. Bly, so I had to spend that whole hour worrying about King, too.

Usually Mrs. Bly's class is my favorite part of the week. She lets us do pretty much anything we want to, as long as it involves art. This week she'd brought in a whole bunch of different colors of clay for us to sculpt with.

I took some red-brown clay that was pretty close to the color of King's fur and sat down on a stool at one of the high tables in the art room. Sunshine was pouring in the big windows all along the walls. Mrs. Bly says that "natural light" is the best for "creating art" so she always leaves the blinds open. The room smelled like paint and chalk and glue. There's a bulletin board for each grade, so you can see the best finger paintings from the kindergartners all the way up to the best photographs and watercolors by the sixth graders. Mrs. Bly changes them all every couple of weeks so everyone gets a chance to be on display.

But the fifth-grade bulletin board almost always has something on it by Pippa Browning, Rosie's best friend. This week it was a colored pencil drawing of Rosie's puppy, Buttons, wrestling with a long pink ribbon. The board was right next to my table, so I looked at it for a while as I rolled the clay around in my hands. I wondered if my rocket ship on Mars painting might be up there the next week. I knew it wouldn't be my *Voyager* drawing; I'd barely had time to work on it at home, what with all the time I had to spend on King instead.

Pippa sat down across from me, holding some dark purple clay. Her long, pale blond hair was clipped back on the sides with turquoise butterfly barrettes, and then pulled back into a ponytail so it wouldn't get in the clay. Her clip-on earrings were silver lace daisies with a blue stone in the middle. She was wearing an apron over her navy blue sweater, too.

Mrs. Bly has aprons for everyone, but I always forget to wear mine.

"That's a really good drawing," I said to Pippa. I pointed at the sketch of Buttons.

"Thanks," she said, turning pink. She poked her clay for a minute without looking up. "Um — so, what are you making, Charlie?"

"I'm trying to do a sculpture of my new dog," I said. "He's a dachshund. His name is King. He's awesome." *Well, most of the time.* "But it's hard to make such a long body stay up on these stubby legs." I hadn't even started on the head because the body kept caving in.

"Maybe try making the body less thin," Pippa suggested. She watched me muddle around with the clay, squashing it this way and that with my fingers. "And, um . . . you could spread the paws out a bit more. For balance. I mean, if you want to." She ducked her head and went back to her own sculpture.

"Hey, that worked," I said five minutes later. My sculpture didn't look as sleek and graceful as King's actual body, but at least it was standing up without collapsing in the middle. I started working on a separate ball of clay for the head. "Thanks, Pippa."

She turned pink again. "Sure."

"What are you making?" I asked.

"I'm not sure yet," she said. "Maybe an elephant."

"Cool."

Her fingers were really thin and they moved quickly as she pressed and shaped the clay. I could see perfect elephant ears appearing already.

"Hey," I said, "can I ask your opinion about something?"

She looked up and blinked at me. I pulled out my sketch pad and tried to draw the mysterious gray thing King had found. "What do you think this is?" I asked her.

Pippa put down her clay and leaned over to peer at the drawing. "Um," she said. "A — maybe a — maybe . . . is it . . ." She turned an even brighter shade of pink. "I'm sorry, Charlie. I think you're a really good artist! I just don't recognize it. Maybe it's the angle . . ."

"Oh, no, I have no idea what it is either," I said. "It's something King found and brought to me."

Pippa exhaled and shook her head so her ponytail slipped over her shoulder. "Oh thank goodness," she said. "I felt so bad!"

"I'm just trying to figure it out," I said. "He also brought me this." I drew the silver cone thing. "They don't *look* important," I said. "But they might be my brother's." I told her about how mad David had been the night before. "It's weird, though, right?" I said. "Why would he be so mad about things like this?"

"Maybe they're parts of something," Pippa said thoughtfully. "Like, something he's building? Does he build things?"

"David? No way," I said. "He lies on his bed snoring or playing video games."

"Oh," Pippa said. "Because I was thinking, maybe he got so mad because he can't finish building whatever it is without these pieces. You know, like when you're trying to make a sundae but there's no chocolate sauce or whipped cream."

I laughed. "That is the worst," I said, and she smiled. "I could believe David building a sundae," I added, "but not something with mysterious gray and silver parts. Maybe they're not his after all. Maybe he's missing something else."

"Why don't you just show those to him and ask him?" Pippa suggested. "He can't be mad at you for something your dog did."

"Oh, yes he can!" I said. "I'd rather give them back without getting yelled at, if possible."

Pippa nodded. "I don't like getting yelled at either," she said. I wondered how she handled being best friends with Rosie. I'd never seen Rosie get mad at Pippa, but she sure yelled about a lot of other things. Rosie's brothers were all pretty loud, too; I'd seen them hollering at Danny during our baseball games.

Pippa went back to her clay elephant, and I finished my sculpture of King. When Mrs. Bly came by to see how we were doing, she was very pleased to find out I'd made something besides a spaceship. Although I might have had better luck making an alien . . . even I had to admit that my dachshund looked more like an elephant itself. Pippa's elephant was exactly right, of course. Mrs. Bly ooooohed at it for a while and showed it to the rest of the class while Pippa turned pink again.

"Good luck figuring out what those pieces are," she said to me as we left class. I could see Rosie and her mom waiting in the parking lot for her, in the car right behind Giovanni and Aidan.

Giovanni winked at me as I got in the backseat. "Who's your cute little friend?" he asked.

"Who?" I said. "Pippa? She's just a girl in my class."

"When a girl plays with her hair that much," Giovanni declared, "it means she likes you. You should bring her flowers next week."

"Giovanni!" I said, and both Aidan and I started laughing. Giovanni thinks all of us should have girlfriends, even Aidan, who thinks girls are scary. But none of my friends were interested in girls, as far as I knew. How weird would it be if I suddenly asked Pippa out? Plus she would definitely say no.

"She doesn't *like* me like that," I said. "She's just Pippa. She always plays with her hair, because she's shy."

"Of course she likes you!" Giovanni said. If he hadn't been driving, he'd have waved his hands around the way he always does when we talk about this. "You're the most handsome boy in the school!"

"What about me?" Aidan asked.

"All right," said Giovanni, "the most handsome boy in the fifth grade." Aidan grinned.

"OK, I think I'm embarrassed enough," I said. "Can we talk about something else?"

"David and Harper went out with Bowser *again*," Aidan said in hushed tones, like he was telling me about a pair of vampires wandering through our yard.

"He said he was too mad at us to stay inside the house where we could ease-drop on them."

"Eavesdrop," Giovanni corrected him.

"That's what I said," Aidan said, nodding. "I told him I would never ease-drop, especially since I know Harper wants to talk about her mom and dad getting divorced, and it's none of my beeswax." He looked unhappy. "But that only made him more mad."

"I wonder why," I said, and Giovanni chuckled. I guess Aidan's snooping wasn't just on me. But if it drove David out of the house, that sure made my life easier.

I hurried upstairs as soon as we got home. This time King heard me coming and wriggled out from under the bed. It turned out I was right to worry so much. He sat down right in the middle of my bright red rug, wagging his tail and sniffing something small and black that definitely didn't belong to either of us.

"King!" I hissed, shutting the door quickly behind me. "What if Aidan had come in first? Or what if David had walked by earlier and seen you with that? You might have ended up on a hot-dog bun!"

King wagged his tail some more. He didn't look

very concerned about the prospect of being eaten by David and Bowser.

I peeked out into the hall. David had closed his door firmly while he was out. He'd also put up a sign with KEEP OUT! scrawled in huge spiky black letters.

Still, King could have stolen this piece earlier in the day, while Bowser was going in and out of the room. I turned it over in my hand. It did look like a piece of something, as Pippa had suggested. It looked a little bit like a tiny fan, like the ones Mrs. Bly puts in the windows of the art room during the summer.

This mystery was too big for me. It was time to call in backup.

CHAPTER 14

I got the phone from Mom's room, lifted King onto the bed with me, and dialed.

The phone rang about seven times before Satoshi picked up.

"Dude!" he said before I could say more than "hi." "This is Midori's cello practice time! You're not supposed to call while she's having a lesson!"

"This is an emergency," I said. "Plus, come on, you guys are always busy with something. There's no way I can keep track."

He lowered his voice. "OK, I'm in the pantry," he said. "Talk quick."

"King did it *again*!" I said. "This is the third time! Now I have *three* weird mystery pieces of something." I retrieved the other two from the hamper and spread them all out on my red and gray striped comforter. There was the first bent gray piece with holes in it. There was the small silver cone-shaped thing. And now there was a little black round bit that looked like a tiny fan. I described them all to Satoshi.

"I have no idea," he said. "It's like only having three pieces of a thousand-piece jigsaw puzzle. How are you supposed to guess? Aw, look, we DO have linguini — I told Mom we did! She always forgets to check behind the rice." I could hear him clattering things around in his pantry.

I wasn't about to let him get distracted, though. "Do you think they're David's?" I asked. "He was really mad at me and Aidan last night. But I don't get it; why would he have little parts like this? All he does is sleep and play video games. It's not like these could be part of a PlayStation or anything. I'd recognize them if they were."

"Have you tried following King?" Satoshi asked. "To see where he goes?"

I looked over at my dog. He was lying wriggled over on his back so I could rub his pale stomach. His ears were flopped over backward. He grinned at me with his pink tongue hanging out.

"He doesn't go anywhere when I'm here," I said. "He waits until I'm gone and then goes exploring. There's no way to catch him in the act because he'd hear me coming."

"Hmmm," said Satoshi. There were more rattling and scrunching sounds coming from his end of the phone. "We have an unreasonable amount of peanut butter in here. And *whoa*, this can of salmon is old."

"Satoshi, would you please focus?" I said. "I need a good —"

"AHA!" Satoshi yelped. "Flour!"

I sighed. "Wow. You have flour. I'm so happy for you."

"No, that's it!" Satoshi said. "That's what you should do! Dip King's paws in flour and then go out the door like you're leaving for a while. When you come back, you can follow his tracks and see where he went!"

I gave King a dubious look. "Do you think that will work?"

"You could try, right?" he said. "And then just sweep it up before your mom gets home."

It sounded better than any of the non-ideas I'd had. "OK, thanks, Satoshi," I said. "I'll give it a shot."

"Let me know what happens!" he said. "But, uh, don't call back before six. If the phone rings again, Midori and Mom and her cello teacher will all yell at me."

I hung up and went downstairs to the kitchen. The bag of flour was already out on the counter because Giovanni was making brownies while Aidan did his homework at the kitchen table. Giovanni gave me a weird look as I poured a little bit of flour into a bowl.

"Uh," Giovanni said. "Something I should know?"

"Just an experiment," I said. "I'll clean it up afterward."

He pushed his glasses up and peered at me. "Nothing's going to explode, right?"

"Oh, probably not," I said, just to see the look on his face.

"An experiment?" Aidan said. "Can I help? Please, can I?"

"No," I said. "This is a one-person experiment." He looked down at his geography homework and kicked the table legs. "But if it works," I added, "I'll tell you what happens."

He nodded, and I took the bowl of flour back upstairs.

"OK, King," I said, lifting him onto the floor. "Now I'm going to go out for a while, so you just be good while I'm gone, OK? And don't worry about this stuff all over your paws. Nothing to see here." He tried to pull away as I dipped his paws in the flour, but by some miracle it didn't spill all over the bedroom floor. When his little brown paws were coated in white, I picked up the bowl and patted his head. "'Bye, King! See you later!"

He stood there sniffing his paws with a bewildered face as I left the room. Although it made me nervous, I cracked David's door open a few inches. The experiment would only work if King had all the same opportunities he usually did for mischief-making.

I made sure to clomp down the stairs so King would hear me leaving. "I'm going outside for a minute!" I called to Giovanni. "I'll just be on the front lawn!"

I shut the front door behind me and then realized that I'd look pretty silly standing there with a bowl of flour if anyone I knew came by. I sat down on the steps, hid the bowl behind a potted plant, and checked my watch. I'd give King ten minutes and then go back in.

Just to be safe, I looked up and down the street, but there was no sign of David and Harper and

Bowser. Maybe they'd gone to the park, like Satoshi had guessed, although they were the least parklike trio I could think of.

Across the street was a family that had just moved in a few weeks ago. They had a boy in sixth grade — I was pretty sure his name was Noah. He was out in his front yard with their little Shetland sheepdog, teaching her to jump through hoops while he held them out in front of him. Her honey-and-white fur flew as she leaped and barked, leaped and barked. She was as barky as King. When Noah saw me sitting on the steps, he waved hello and I waved back.

While I was watching, a girl with long, straight brown hair in a ponytail pulled into his driveway and dropped her bike on the grass. I think it was my baseball coach's daughter Rory; her stepsister Cameron is in Aidan's class. Aidan's a little afraid of Cameron because she can throw a tantrum about the smallest things — I saw her have a screaming fit at his birthday party last year because her ice cream had melted and made her cake all soggy. The Sheltie bounced over and barked at Rory, then ran back to the hoops.

Half a minute later, another girl with reddish hair biked up with an enormous shaggy black dog loping alongside her. I knew she was Heidi Tyler, another sixth-grader. I remembered her because she'd tried to say hi to Bowser a few times, and she didn't even seem flustered by how rude David was to her about it.

The three of them talked for a minute, and then Noah opened his front door and shouted something into the house. He came back with a silver chain leash, which he clipped onto the Sheltie. The three of them set off in the direction of the park with the girls pushing their bikes and both dogs trotting happily beside them.

Man, that guy was popular. It seemed like every time I saw him he was with a different set of friends. I didn't know how he'd made so many friends so quickly, but I guessed from the fact that he always waved to me that he must be pretty cool.

I checked my watch. Ten minutes! Time for the moment of truth.

I ran upstairs to my room just in time to see a waving brown tail disappear under the bed. And sure enough, there were tiny white pawprints all over my floor.

"Let's see what you got this time," I said, crouching down to lift up my comforter. King blinked at me in surprise, like *What, you're back already?* He came wriggling out to lick my nose. I lay down on my stomach and pulled out a little bundle of orange and blue wires attached to some kind of small electronic-looking green rectangle with lots of silver bits on it.

"Uh-oh," I said. "Now this actually looks important."

King puffed out his chest like, *I know, aren't I impressive?*

I gathered the other three mystery items and carried all four of them to the door, following King's pawprints.

They led exactly where I'd feared . . . straight down the hall, into David's room.

CHAPTER 15

O h, *no*," I said. "King! Now we have to go in there!"

Not only did I have to get the pieces back into David's room without him finding out, I also had to clean up the flour tracks that King had left behind in there. Yeah, thanks, Satoshi — that was a *great* idea.

I grabbed a washcloth from the linen closet, got it a little bit wet, and quickly wiped up the prints outside David's door. Then I took a deep breath and pushed the door open.

The room was still a giant mess. Mom's philosophy was, if we kept it in our rooms and she didn't have to see it, she wouldn't nag us about it. But I couldn't imagine how David ever found anything in here. Clothes were piled on chairs and the bed and the desk. Books and papers and video game controllers were scattered over the floor; the game on the TV was paused in the middle of a car chase. And in the center of the room was a cleared space where something was covered with a big white sheet.

King trotted over to this immediately. He'd worn off the flour so his paws weren't leaving tracks anymore, but I could see the prints he'd left before. He gave me a pleased expression like he was glad we were finally co-conspirators on this important mission, and then he nosed at a corner of the sheet until he could duck underneath. His tail stuck up so I could see him wriggling around under there.

"King!" I whispered. "Get back out here! You'll get us in so much trouble!" Of course he paid no attention to me. I bent down and wiped up the flour paw prints as fast as I could. Then I hesitated. David would be *so* mad if he found out I'd been nosing around his room. But I had to replace the pieces, right? And it sure looked like they went under that sheet. So it was only logical for me to take a quick peek . . . and besides, I was absolutely dying of curiosity.

What was David hiding in here? Would this explain the red and white paint on his hands, too? It was like finding a book that everyone said was too grown-up for you, which was the kind of thing that only made me want to read it even more.

I glanced behind me, and then with a quick tug, I threw the sheet aside.

It took a minute for my brain to catch up with what my eyes were seeing.

There was an *airplane* sitting on David's floor. A real, honest-to-goodness airplane, although of course it was small — about the length of Bowser, maybe — and it wasn't totally finished. Miniature parts were scattered around it, including some that matched the ones I was holding. And it was only half painted, in careful brushstrokes of red and white with blue star decals on the wings and tail.

The box it had come in was sitting next to the plane with the instructions neatly folded on top of it. King poked his nose at one of the wings and then looked at me like, *Well, I would have brought you the whole plane, but I'm afraid it doesn't fit in my mouth.* He sat down and wagged his tail. *Pretty cool thing that I found, though, huh?*

I gaped at the whole scene in confusion. I mean, I'd heard of model airplanes, but there was no part of my head that could put together my lazy, mean, boring brother David with something as detailed and painstaking and kind of cool as building a remote-controlled airplane.

I was so bewildered that I didn't hear the front door . . . or the jingling of dog tags . . . or the footsteps coming up the stairs . . . until it was too late.

David's door slammed open.

"What are you doing in my room?" David shouted. "I knew it! I knew you were snooping around my stuff!"

King jumped to his paws and started barking. Behind David, Bowser started barking, too, deep gruff angry barks.

"I'm not snooping!" I cried, yelling to be heard over the dogs. "I promise — I mean — I figured out that it was King who came in and took something, so I was returning it! See?" I held out the pieces of the airplane and David snatched them from my hands.

"I should have known," he snarled. "You keep your stupid dog out of here."

"I was just leaving!" I grabbed King before he could scoop up another airplane piece in his mouth.

"You better!" David said. "And stay out of my room from now on! You and Mr. Meanie-Weenie both!"

"Rrrrrrrrrrrrrrrrr," Bowser growled up at the dog flopped over my arm. King growled back.

David stepped aside so I could leave, but before I'd taken two steps, Harper appeared in the doorway and squeezed by him.

"It's loud in here," she observed. "Dogs need to chill." She started across the room to the paused video game, her long black cardigan flapping around her jean skirt and ripped black stockings.

David gave me a serious *GET OUT* face and dodged toward the sheet. Too late. Harper stopped suddenly and looked down at the uncovered airplane. Her blank face twitched like she was about to express an emotion.

"Wait. That's the big secret?" she asked him.

"It's nothing," David muttered.

I couldn't help it. I paused in the doorway. This was like going behind the scenes of a horror movie and finding out the spooky killers were actually ordinary people. David had his back to me, so he didn't notice that I was still there.

Harper crouched down and brushed the airplane's wings with her fingertips. "You're building an airplane," she said slowly.

"It's just a stupid kit," David said, tugging on Bowser's ears like he wanted to take the plane and throw it out the window. "Come on, let's get back to the game."

"My dad used to make these," Harper said. She sat down on the floor and picked up a wheel, spinning it between her fingers. "You know, back when he wasn't a jerk. Sometimes he let me watch."

David rubbed his head. "Yeah," he said. "I found this in my dad's stuff. I think he was planning to build it with me."

Aha! I thought. *That's why the trunk in the attic was out of place. David must have been going through Dad's old things.*

Harper looked up at him. Behind all the black makeup, her green eyes had this faraway look. "Can I help you finish it?"

"Really?" David fidgeted with his shirt. "You don't have to. If you think it's lame."

"Shut up and hand me a screwdriver," Harper said, and then she cracked the first smile I'd seen from her since sixth grade.

I hurried away as David sat down on the floor beside her. My guess was he'd be furious if he realized I'd seen that. I wondered for the first time if there was something going on with him and Harper that was more than friends hanging out. Maybe I should have thought of that sooner, but the idea of a girl actually *liking* David was about as strange as finding an airplane in his bedroom.

Aidan came into our room a few minutes later, while I was lying on my bed, staring at the ceiling and thinking about this secret other David I'd just discovered.

"Did you see what David and Harper are doing?" I asked him.

He shook his head. "His door is closed." He came over and tried to pat King, but the dachshund dodged away to the other side of me. Aidan rubbed his arms and then gave me a hopeful look. "Want to play cards? Giovanni's been teaching me snap."

"No thanks," I said. I checked my watch; it was after six. "I have to go call Satoshi." I got the phone and went into the attic with King so I could talk without Aidan overhearing me. Midori picked up the phone, too, so I told her and Satoshi about the whole thing, the airplane and Harper and everything.

"Whoa," Midori said. "Maybe that's why David is so grumpy all the time! Maybe he's had this unrequited love for Harper for years but he's been too afraid to do anything about it and it's been eating him up inside! That's so romantic!"

Satoshi snorted. "You watch too many shows on the CW."

"What's unrequited?" I asked.

"You guys are hopeless," Midori said. "Get off the phone so I can call Michelle and talk to her about it."

"You can't tell her!" I said. "What if it gets back to David? He might kill me!"

"Michelle isn't Cadence Bly," said Midori. "She can keep a secret."

"Midori!"

"All RIGHT," she said. "I'll change all the names to protect the guilty. Which is you, just to be clear."

After we got off the phone, I stayed up in the attic playing hide-and-seek with King until dinnertime. It was totally hilarious — of course he wouldn't sit and stay, so I had to pin his leash under my crate of books to keep him in one place while I went and hid the giraffe somewhere in the attic. Then I'd let him off the leash and tell him to "find it!" and he'd race around the attic, sniffing under furniture and digging through piles of fabric and sticking his nose behind all the trunks until he finally popped out with the giraffe in his mouth, looking like he'd just won a Nobel Prize for Finding Giraffes.

"Charlie!" Aidan called from downstairs. "Dinner's ready!"

As I turned off my lamp, I heard the front door slam. I peeked out the window at our front lawn.

Harper and David were walking down our drive to the sidewalk together. But that wasn't the weird part.

The weird part was . . . they were holding hands.

CHAPTER 16

You couldn't tell right away that David was in a better mood than usual. He wouldn't speak to me at dinner, and when Giovanni asked him what was up, he grumbled something about how "Mr. Meanie-Weenie" was a "nosy, snooping thief," and when Aidan politely asked for the mashed potatoes, David practically threw the bowl at him.

But a couple of times I caught David staring down at his plate with a weird almost-smile on his face. And there were a few moments when he would normally have jumped into the conversation with something really mean, but it was like he'd spaced out and forgotten his lines. He wasn't even all that rude about asking to be excused, and the music coming from his room when I went upstairs later actually sounded like real music, not people screaming into microphones.

I finished my homework while Aidan lay on the floor drawing dinosaurs and King snoozed on my pillows. I wondered if there was any way I could get David to show me his airplane once it was finished. I had so many questions about how he'd built it! Most of all, I really, really wanted to see it fly.

"Want to see my dinosaurs?" Aidan asked as I closed my math book. "I've been practicing! You can actually tell this is an allosaurus now, I think."

"Yeah, that's great," I said, glancing at the sheet of paper in front of him. "Don't forget to brush your teeth before Mom comes in to say good night." I climbed into bed and picked up *The Witches* from my nightstand. King scrambled up the bed and went *dig, dig, dig* in the covers until he'd arranged a little nest beside me. He lay down with a happy snort and rested his chin on my lap.

"Maybe I should get a dog, too," Aidan said with a wistful look at King.

"Yeah, I bet King would *love* to deal with another dog in the house," I said. "Besides, you already have Meowser."

Aidan picked up the black-and-white cow-spotted pajamas Giovanni had left out for him. "It's not the same," he said, wandering out the door to the bathroom.

Mom poked her head in a few minutes later. "Hey guys," she said. "Does anyone know why I found a bowl of flour outside behind my begonias?"

"Oops," I said. "That was me. Um. Long story."

She raised her eyebrows. "OK, I won't ask."

She forgot to tell me to put King on the floor, so I let him sleep next to me on the bed. It wasn't like he took up much space, and he didn't snore nearly as loud as Aidan did, and she never said anything about Meowser sleeping on Aidan's bed. Besides, I kind of liked feeling him curled up against my back while I fell asleep.

I didn't see David again until the next afternoon. He was already gone when Giovanni woke us up — Giovanni said he'd muttered something about walking to school, which didn't sound like David at all. But then, neither did model airplanes and a raccoon-eyed girlfriend.

It was after school, and I was up in the attic trying (again) to make King sit, when I heard the front door slam in David's loud, grumpy way. I waited about ten minutes, and then I carried King downstairs and checked out one of the back windows.

David and Bowser were out in the backyard, just the two of them. David was throwing sticks for Bowser, which was pretty funny because Bowser would start to chase them while they were in the air, but once they hit the ground he'd stop and look confused like, *Wait, where'd it go? Why isn't it flying anymore?*

I took a deep breath. I was probably about to get yelled at. But there was a part of me that really wanted to talk to mysterious Other David, especially about the plane he'd built.

Aidan was in the kitchen helping Giovanni fold laundry when I went through.

"Hi Charlie!" he chirped. "Look, we washed your shirt! Good as new! See?" He held up my CHARLIE shirt, the one he'd worn on my birthday. It looked like it had been scrubbed and polished so all the colors were bright as the day I'd bought it.

"He made me put it through twice," Giovanni said, shaking his head with a smile. "Using every stain remover in the laundry room."

"Oh," I said. "Thanks, Aidan." *For washing the shirt* you *got dirty*. "It looks great."

"Where are you going?" he asked.

"Nowhere," I said, pulling on the sliding door.

"Watch out," he said. "David and Bowser are out there."

"I know," I said. I let King scoot out the door ahead of me, and then I closed it behind us and walked down the deck steps to the grass.

David saw me coming and scowled. "Did I miss a presidential announcement?" he said. "Is this Annoy David to Death Week and nobody told me?"

"I wanted to say I'm sorry again," I said bravely. "I feel bad about King going in your room, and I really didn't mean to touch your stuff."

"You *should* feel bad," he said, snapping a branch between his hands.

I paused. "Um," I said. "That airplane looked really cool."

"I don't want to talk about it," David said. "You'd better take Mr. Meanie-Weenie back inside before he gets in Bowser's way."

Now I was mad again. "Stop calling him that! King is *not* mean!" I said. "Bowser is the one who's mean! He's mean and he hates everybody, just like you!"

"I don't hate everybody!" David snapped. "Just annoying little brothers who can't mind their own business!"

"Fine!" I said. "I was just trying to be nice! I just wanted to say that your plane looked cool, that's all! You don't have to be such a jerk about it!" I turned my back on him. "Come on, King, we're not wanted h —"

I stopped midsentence. OK, I'd thought David and Harper holding hands was the weirdest thing I'd see all week. But that was nothing compared to what was happening in our backyard right at that moment.

King and Bowser were galloping around the yard together. It was hard to tell who was chasing who — it was like they kept switching places. One would stop and spin around and do a play bow, wagging his tail. Then the other would pounce at his head, and the first one would go tearing off across the lawn with the second in hot pursuit. Then they'd switch and do the same thing in reverse. King's ears were flapping like seagull wings and his stubby legs pumped madly over the grass, but he had no trouble keeping up with Bowser.

And Bowser was acting like he'd been possessed by some kind of adorable puppy. His mouth was hanging open and his tongue flopped out as he romped around, spinning and leaping and wagging his tail.

I glanced over at David. His face looked as astonished as I felt. We just stood there staring at the two dogs for a long moment.

Then I heard a sound from David that I hadn't heard in ages. It took me a moment to figure out that he was laughing. He doubled over and I started laughing, too.

"Look at them!" David said through tears of laughter. Bowser raced right past us with King at his heels. "Who *are* you?" David asked Bowser, but his dog was having too much fun to stop and pay attention.

David sat down on the grass to watch, and after a moment, I did, too. I figured he didn't seem as mad at me anymore, and it was too funny watching the dogs play with each other. I couldn't believe it. I tried to think if we'd ever let them out in the yard together before. So far they'd only seen each other in the house, or on leashes. Maybe they just needed enough space to run around in order to figure out that they could actually play together. Or maybe they both felt like they had to defend the territory where the food was, but out here they could relax and be friends.

Whatever the reason, it was pretty awesome. David and I sat there watching them for at least twenty minutes before they got tired. And even then you could tell they both wanted to keep playing. They were lying down facing each other and panting like crazy, but whenever one of them twitched, the other would snap to attention in case it was time to play again. Bowser flopped over in the grass first. This was probably more exercise than he'd had in his whole life.

David rubbed his head and looked at me sideways. "OK, wait here," he said suddenly.

He got up and went inside. While he was gone, I filled the outside dish with water so both dogs could get a drink. King licked my hand and rubbed his wet snout against my wrist as if he was saying, *Gee boss, this was fun. Where'd this nice dog come from? Why don't we do this every day?* Even Bowser wagged his tail at me a little bit.

I looked up as the sliding door opened and David came out. He was carrying the plane and the remote controller that went with it.

I just barely managed not to jump up and yell "HOORAY!" the way Aidan totally would have done.

"Wow," I said as David walked over to me. "That is — really, really cool." The plane looked all put together and perfect. I guess he'd finished it with Harper the day before.

"It *is* kind of cool, huh?" David said, holding it up and studying it proudly.

"I can't believe you built it," I said. "The whole thing? By yourself? How did you even know what to do?"

"Well, there were instructions," he said. "But it was pretty hard. I've been working on it for a while." He turned it over to check the underside. "I'm sure it would have been easier with Dad's help."

I wasn't sure what to say to that, so I settled for "Yeah."

"This was in his stuff," David explained. "You probably don't remember, but he built things all the time. He was great at explaining what he was doing while I watched him. He was always talking about turning half of the garage into a woodworking studio one day."

"Really?" I said. I'd never known that about my dad, but it was cool to imagine him sawing and sanding and hammering things together. "Maybe you should do that. I bet Mom would let you. It looks like you're good at building things, like he was." I nodded at the plane.

"Hmm," David said. "Maybe I should. Harper seemed kind of into it, too."

I decided not to ask if she was his girlfriend now. I was afraid that might send the conversation in a grumpy direction. "And the good news is," I said instead, "if you're working in the garage, King won't be able to get in to steal parts of your projects."

David actually laughed. "Good point," he said. "Want to see it fly?"

"Yeah!" I said. "Kind of desperately!"

He grinned, and I had a weird feeling like I'd fallen through time and run into a much younger, nicer David, like he used to be when he was my age. I always forget about that David, because the one in the present day is so much bigger and more real.

David flew the plane around the yard and above the trees and in circles all around us. Bowser and King barked and tried to jump at it every time the plane flew low enough, which was really funny, but David kept it out of their reach. He even let me work the remote controller for a minute or two, and I didn't crash the plane into anything, so that was sort of awesome and surprising.

"Do you think you could build a rocket, maybe?" I asked as I handed the controller back. "You know, like the ones on TV that shoot straight up in the air and come down on a little parachute?"

David shrugged, steering the plane around a tall tree. "Yeah, I probably could," he said. "I'd just need a kit."

"Well, if you did," I said, "and if you ever needed help with it, I could, like . . . help you with that. I mean . . . if you wanted to." I was trying not to let on how exciting that would be. Building our own rocket! Maybe Mom would get us a kit for Christmas if I convinced her that David and I could build it together.

"Maybe," David said vaguely. He swooped the plane down low across the grass and King leaped to his paws, barking wildly at it as it shot over his head.

"You know," David said with a laugh. "King really is kind of a silly name for that dog."

I sighed and finally admitted what I'd been thinking for three days. "He doesn't seem to like it, either," I said. "He never comes when I call him."

"Well, that just takes practice," David said, his eyes fixed on the plane above us. "It took about a hundred treats before Bowser figured out his name. But King is a name for a German shepherd or a Dalmatian, not a wiener dog."

"I'm not calling him Mr. Meanie-Weenie," I said.

David laughed a little, but not in a mean way. "Sure," he said. "But there must be something in between. Earl of Mustard or something."

"Yeah, I can just see myself yelling 'EARL OF MUSTARD!' across the park," I said.

"Hot Dog Duke," David mused.

"Emperor Wiener," I suggested.

"I know!" David said. "You should call him Lord Sausage."

I laughed. I actually kind of liked that. But I still couldn't imagine shouting it across the yard when I wanted him to come inside. "That's not bad," I said. "But maybe in front of people I'll keep calling him King for short."

David shrugged. "Yeah, I guess that's a bit more normal."

I wasn't crazy enough to think that this meant David and I were best friends now. I was sure he'd be grumpy about something else before long. I knew I would accidentally make him mad, or Harper would break up with him, or King would get on his nerves, and rotten, scary David would come out again.

But one thing had changed. King and Bowser were friends now. They might still growl at each other inside, but if we let them outside together, I was sure we'd see a lot more romping and playing like what had happened today. And if that made David even a tiny bit happier, then there was hope that every once in a while I'd get to hang out with cool David, too.

I grinned at King, who was asleep with his ears flopped out on the grass on either side of his head. Who knew that the best part of having my own dog would be the part where he made friends with someone else?

CHAPTER 17

When we finally headed back inside, I saw Aidan watching us through the glass doors. He was sitting at the table pretending to do homework by the time we got inside, though. King and Bowser trotted straight to their food bowls and gobbled up what was there. The kitchen smelled like Giovanni's special meat lasagna. He says it's a recipe handed down from his grandmother, but I've seen him reading the instructions off the pasta box.

David went upstairs with the plane. I stopped to wash my hands at the kitchen sink. Aidan kept his head bent over his worksheets.

"Charlie, can I talk to you for a minute?" Giovanni asked, waving me into the living room. When I followed him in there, he glanced behind me to make sure Aidan couldn't see us, and then lowered his voice. "I found something a little odd in the laundry," he said.

Whoops. I looked at the dented, chewed-up thing in his hands and winced. I'd totally forgotten about Aidan's triceratops.

"I think I can guess what happened here," Giovanni said wryly. "What I want to know is what you're going to do about it."

"Buy him a new one?" I said. "I could give it to him for his birthday next week. Mom always gives us twenty dollars each to spend on presents for each other."

Giovanni looked disappointed in me. "So for his present you'll give him something he already had — until your dog destroyed it. Is that what you'd want for your birthday?"

I shuffled my sneakers on the rug. "I guess not."

"I think replacing it is a good idea, though," Giovanni said, patting my shoulder. "I know you've been saving your allowance. Right?"

Yeah, for a telescope, I thought. But I knew Giovanni was right, and it wouldn't cost very much to buy a plastic dinosaur. I'd come up with something else for Aidan's birthday.

"OK," I said.

"Aidan has chess club after school on Friday," Giovanni said. "We can go to the toy store then and get a new dinosaur and his birthday presents at the same time."

"Thanks, Giovanni," I said. "Do I have to show him what happened to this one?"

Giovanni thought for a moment. "If he hasn't noticed it's missing yet," he said, "then I think you can wait until you have the new one to replace it." He gave me the ruined toy. "Dinner will be ready in an hour."

I ran upstairs to the attic and hid the triceratops in one of the old trunks under some lacy napkins. Then I went back down to my room and found King snoozing on the red rug. I sat down on the floor and scratched behind his ears. I knew I should probably start my Spanish homework, but he looked so peaceful snuggled up next to my knees that I didn't want to move and wake him up.

Just as I thought that, though, Aidan burst into the room and King sprang to his paws, blinking and staring about like he was wondering where the fire was.

"Aw, you woke him up," I said, patting King's back.

Aidan looked contrite. "I'm sorry," he said. "I just finished my homework so I thought maybe I'd come up and see if you wanted to play cards or watch a video or look at my dinosaur drawings or —"

"I can't," I said. I climbed to my feet and picked up my Spanish workbook. "I'm going up to the attic to start my homework."

Aidan crouched down on the floor and held out his hand to King. "I'm sorry, King," he said. "I didn't mean to wake you."

King lifted his nose like he couldn't be bothered sniffing Aidan's hand. He backed up and strutted in a wide circle around Aidan to follow me to the door.

"I wish he would let me say hi to him," Aidan said, sitting back on his heels.

"He's a little particular," I said. "He chooses his friends carefully."

"Yeah," Aidan said quietly. "I guess it makes sense that King doesn't like me any more than you do."

I stopped in my tracks. What Aidan had said was almost exactly what I'd said about Bowser to David — except Aidan's was a much nicer version.

Suddenly I felt really, really terrible. Waves of guilt crashed over my head.

All this time I'd been thinking about how awful David was to me — and I'd never even noticed that I was being just as awful to my own little brother. He just wanted me to hang out with him, and instead I kept avoiding him or ignoring him.

Was that what Aidan thought . . . that I was as mean as David? Worse yet . . . was I?

I backed up and put my Spanish book down on my desk. "Actually," I said, "I can do this after dinner. You want to come up to the attic with me?"

Aidan's head popped up. He gave me a disbelieving, hopeful look. "You — seriously? You mean it?"

"Sure," I said. "I can show you the game Satoshi and Midori and I played with King. We figured out a way to make him like them. I bet it would work with you, too."

Aidan scrambled to his feet. "Really? There's a way to make King like me?"

King was standing in the doorway wagging his tail. "Well, we can try!" I said. "But I don't see why not." I grinned at Aidan. "I mean, everybody *else* likes you."

He ducked his head. "Not everybody!" But I could see the smile he was trying to hide.

I grabbed King's toys and treats and we climbed up into the attic together. Aidan looked around with wide eyes, and I realized he hadn't been up here in a really long time.

"Want to see something cool?" I said. "This box is full of photo albums from when we were little." I dragged it over to the window and pulled out the one on top. I knew it was the one with the first photos of Aidan. "Look what a goofball you were," I said, pointing at a photo of Aidan with a sheet tied around his shoulders like a cape. He was posed like a superhero about to leap off the couch. "Acting funny for the camera."

Aidan sat down on the beanbag next to me as I turned the page. "And here's you with Dad," I said. "Your first Halloween. Hey, I remember that!" I suddenly had a really clear memory of Dad's big hand holding mine as we walked from house to house with my Buzz Lightyear pants flapping around my boots. "You couldn't believe that we could just knock on doors and get candy. You wanted to knock on doors for candy for, like, a month after that."

Aidan giggled. "Who's that?" he asked, pointing at a photo on the next page. I peered at it, and then I started laughing.

"That's David!" I said. The photo was of seven-year-old David in the garden with Mom. He was wearing one of her floppy sun hats and waving at the camera. Behind him were a row of bulbs and a trowel.

Aidan started laughing, too. "That's how he knew they were daffodils!" he said. "He used to help Mom garden just like I do!"

"I totally don't remember that," I said. "We should keep it in mind next time he teases us."

"Yeah," Aidan said with a delighted grin.

King poked his nose under my arm to find out why we were paying attention to something that wasn't him.

"Sorry, King," I said. "Here, Aidan, you give him a treat. He really likes these." I showed Aidan how to hold his hand flat and near the ground. "Stay still so he'll come close to you."

King sniffed the air, blinked at Aidan, and then looked at me like, *Really? This guy? Are you sure this is a good idea?*

"Go on, King," I said. "Good boy. Good dog."

He licked one of his paws, and then he took a dainty step forward and slurped the treat off of Aidan's hand.

"Yay!" Aidan said. "He did it!"

"Do that a few more times," I said, packing the

album away again. "I'll go hide his toys so we can play hide-and-seek. And maybe later, if he'll come to you, we can practice teaching him his name."

"Really?" Aidan said. He looked like he still couldn't believe I was really talking to him. "You don't mind if I play with him?"

"I don't want to be like David," I said. "I think Bowser would be happier if he could play with the rest of us. Did you see him with King out in the yard?"

Aidan nodded. "That was so funny!"

"King loved it, too," I said, "and I want him to be able to play like that with other people." I stroked King's smooth brown head. "As long as you still like me best, Lord Sausage." He thumped his tail on the attic floor and gave me an adoring look.

Aidan cracked up. "Lord Sausage! That's awesome!"

"It was David's suggestion," I admitted. "I've decided it's King's secret code name."

"I won't tell anyone," Aidan promised. He took another treat out of the bag and held it out. "Here, King," he said. "Who's a good dog?"

King turned away from me to investigate the treat, and I snuck off to hide the giraffe and the zebra.

When I looked back from behind the mirror, I saw Aidan laughing as King licked his whole hand clean.

King was still my dog. Sharing him with Aidan or even Bowser wouldn't change that. And if he helped me to remember how to be a good brother, then he'd already be making our house a more fun place for everyone. There was no chance Mom would send him away once she realized that.

Besides, if I had to admit it, hanging out with Aidan was actually not that bad.

King noticed that I was gone and whirled around, searching the attic with his shining dark eyes. His long brown ears swung back and forth as he looked for me. I tucked the giraffe into the corner of a bookshelf and jumped out into the open so my dog could see me.

"OK, King!" I called, spreading my arms. "Come find it!"

Read them all!

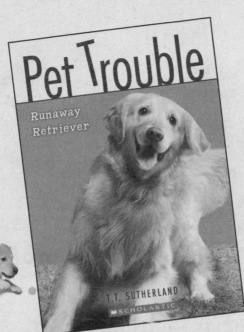

Pet Trouble
Runaway Retriever
T.T. SUTHERLAND
SCHOLASTIC

Runaway Retriever

Merlin is a great dog.

Parker's new golden retriever is a guy's best friend, with tons of
energy for walks and playing catch. And Merlin clearly thinks
Parker is the best thing since rawhide bones.

There's just one thing . . .

Merlin is an escape artist. No fence is too high, no cage too
strong to keep him from following Parker everywhere he goes.
Can Parker make Merlin sit—and *stay*?

Loudest Beagle on the Block

Trumpet is a great dog.

Ella spends all her time inside, practicing her music for the school talent show. But with her new beagle, Trumpet, she's starting to make new friends and see a whole world away from the piano bench.

There's just one thing . . .

Every time Ella starts to sing, Trumpet howls. Loudly. If Ella doesn't lose her canine costar, she doesn't stand a chance at the show—but can tone-deaf Trumpet tone it down?

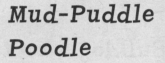

Mud-Puddle Poodle

Buttons is a great dog.

When she finally gets a dog of her own, Rosie knows it's going to be perfect—unlike everything else in her chaotic house with four crazy brothers.

There's just one thing . . .

Buttons hates her fancy dog pillow, but she loves a good, dirty pile of leaves! Rosie's new pet is her complete opposite. Can she ever learn to to live with this mess of a dog?

Pet Trouble

Mud-Puddle Poodle

T.T. SUTHERLAND

SCHOLASTIC

Bulldog Won't Budge

Meatball is a great dog.

Eric has always wanted a dog, so when a bulldog named
Meatball is abandoned at his mother's veterinarian office, Eric
is sure it's fate—he can give Meatball a new home!

There's just one thing . . .

Meatball is stubborn. And slow. Eric wants to go to the park
and play fetch, but Meatball likes to lie in the grass and drool.
Is there anything Eric can do to get this bulldog to budge?

Oh No, Newf!

Yeti is a great dog.

Heidi is dog-crazy. So when she finds a friendly, abandoned Newfoundland, she's determined to take care of him. Even if her parents have forbidden her from bringing a dog home, she'll find a way—by keeping Yeti in her friend's shed!

There's just one thing . . .

Yeti is sweet, and Heidi wants to give him a real home. But he's also enormous and clumsy, and basically her parents' worst nightmare. Can Heidi turn him into a model dog? Or is Yeti just too big to handle?

Smarty-Pants Sheltie

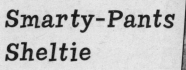

Jeopardy is a great dog.

Noah's family just moved, and Noah is nervous about starting a new school with new people. At least he can distract himself with the family's Shetland sheepdog, Jeopardy. Noah's mom suggests a dog agility class, which seems like an OK idea—at first.

There's just one thing . . .

Jeopardy is so embarrassing! When Noah takes her to class, she barks, runs away, and doesn't listen to him at all. Noah wants to make friends, not get laughed at chasing around this crazy dog! How will he ever fit in with this shouty Sheltie?

Bad to the
Bone Boxer

Tombo is a great dog.

Michelle loves her new boxer, Tombo. He's cute and energetic, and Michelle can't wait to play with him and her best friend's poodle puppy, Buttons.

There's just one thing . . .

Tombo likes to chew things. A LOT. He's destroying everything—furniture, clothes, shoes, and maybe even Michelle's relationship with her BFF. Michelle knows Tombo doesn't want to be bad . . . but is there any way to make him good?

For more magical fun, be sure to
check out these tails of enchantment!